DOCTOR WHO

ROGUE

ROGUE

Based on the BBC television adventure

KATE HERRON
& BRIONY REDMAN

BOOKS

BBC Books, an imprint of Ebury Publishing
20 Vauxhall Bridge Road
London SW1V 2SA

BBC Books is part of the Penguin Random House group of companies whose
addresses can be found at global.penguinrandomhouse.com

Doctor Who is produced in Wales by Bad Wolf
with BBC Studios Productions.

Executive Producers: Russell T Davies, Julie Gardner,
Jane Tranter, Joel Collins & Phil Collinson

First published by BBC Books in 2024

www.penguin.co.uk

A CIP catalogue record for this book is available from the British Library

ISBN 9781785948831

Editorial Director: Albert DePetrillo
Project Editor: Steve Cole
Cover Design: Two Associates
Cover illustration: Dan Liles

Typeset by Rocket Editorial Ltd

Printed and bound in Great Britain by Clays Ltd, Elcograf S.p.A.

The authorised representative in the EEA is Penguin Random House Ireland,
Morrison Chambers, 32 Nassau Street, Dublin D02 YH68

Contents

For the ones we have loved

Chapter 1
Rogue

Gurgle, in some corners of the universe, was considered a drink for unimaginative beings. But this never hindered or stopped their aggressive advertising campaigns over the millennia.

Want that new corner-office job? Drink Gurgle. Want to marry your crush from Thursday's book club? Drink Gurgle. Accidentally drove your Jetzopod 345 into a tree? Probably drink some Gurgle because, if this has happened, you have set yourself on fire and will need to cool down a bit.

There were hundreds of planets dedicated to the manufacturing of the drink, and the planet Glarcom was one of these. Hundreds of beings flocked there, all with the hope of finding work in one of Gurgle's many factories. In return for their hard work they would be given living quarters for free and, after 500 years of service, a less than average pension, but it's the memories that matter. Plus, who needs health care when you have Gurgle's Vittamine to charge up those old bones?

One morning on Glarcom, the employees of Gurgle were all frantically making their way to work. Aliens of every shape and size, all crammed into the shiny chrome-green transport trains. They were all wearing the same green suit, with a grey tie. The Gurgle logo was liberally splashed across it.*

Amongst the crowd sat a man. No bag by his feet and in his hands he gripped a plastic entry card. A ballpoint pen with a large 'G' stuck out of the top of his suit pocket. He looked preoccupied, something bigger and better than a day at a fizzy drink factory on his mind.

He looked out of the window at Glarcom City coming into view as the train snaked past multiple high-rises which fell away to reveal large industrial factories, spewing out green smoke into the muddy polluted sky. Projected on the buildings was Gurgle's most recent advert. It was of a muscular alien man lifting a can of Gurgle to his mouth. He was enjoying the drink so much that it spilled from his face and down onto his green biceps. A slogan

---

* Tan France would be shaken.

flashed up across him: 'Perfection never tasted this good.'

The man on the train smirked. Sure, perfection. He'd drunk poison that was more nutritious than Gurgle.

'It's great, isn't it?' The purple one-eyed alien sitting next to the man was grinning. 'I used to think we'd never beat the current taste, but we did it again.'

The man smiled at him and nodded, sure. He didn't want to make any enemies here. It was clear that charm came easily to him, even in the early sweaty hours of the morning commute.

Suddenly a loud horn sounded, and the train pulled into Glarcom City. There was a shift of mood in the carriage; everyone leapt up off the seats as the doors whizzed open. There was a chorus of shoving, kicking and shouting.

The man struggled out of his seat and found himself almost carried by the bustling crowd as they all moved towards the cruelly narrow exit doors. Eventually wiggling through and removing a co-worker's elbow from his chest, he felt the bright sunlight hit his face. Phew. He was finally outside, but then came the smell of something sickly…

Right ahead, he saw the source. A fountain. It was a pastel-green carving of a small green alien, Hexham Droogle. The founder of Gurgle. Droogle was laughing hysterically.

The man scoffed; *I guess when you're that rich you're always laughing*, he thought. In each of Droogle's small green carved hands was a carved supersized can of Gurgle that *actual* Gurgle splashed out of. It was hitting the concrete and slowly being cooked by the sun. It stank.

The man held his breath and walked past, the smell of toffee intensifying the closer he got, and went into a large green-glass building, Gurgle's headquarters.

Inside was a large foyer. It was relatively stripped back. The walls and floor were a pastel yellow marble contrasting with a green desk in the centre of the room. Behind this sat a receptionist, who smiled sweetly as they muttered good morning again and again like they were saying it for the first time, each time.

On either side of the desk were turnstiles, hundreds of turnstiles, as far as the eye could see. The man approached and, as he had watched the others do, he tapped his ID on the screen. Instead of the bright purple light granting him entry, however, it flashed orange and made a strange sound. It didn't take more than a second for the workers behind to start complaining.

The man turned back and flashed a very charming smile then tapped his card again. Nope. The same sound and orange light.

There was a loud sigh beside him, and the man watched as a large hippo-like alien in a Gurgle Security cap walked over.

'All right, what's wrong?' he grumbled.

The man smiled apologetically. 'I thought this would—'

The guard grunted, 'Number?'

'46731,' said the man. He could feel his heartbeat getting faster but was determined to keep his cool.

The guard rummaged around in his pocket and pulled out a tiny device. He began to tap through it slowly. It clearly wasn't designed for the type of alien the guard was and his large grey fingers regularly hit the wrong buttons. He cursed. Multiple times.

The man, smiled, trying to keep the mood pleasant. 'It's my first day.'

Not even a grin from the guard, who continued to wrestle with his screen. The man looked at the alien's large fists, aware he could easily squash him in an instant.

Behind the man, the crowd of frustrated Gurgle workers was only growing. Sensing a scene forming, the man quietly moved his hands towards his jacket pocket. No one noticed him do this, and there was something in there he needed. His hands twitched, ready to grab, then … the guard sighed. He pulled out his own card and tapped it on the turnstile.

'Just go through, newbie. Get that card fixed. I ain't got the energy.'

The man took a breath: *phew!* He moved his hand out of his pocket and ruffled his hair. He smiled that same charming smile he had given the alien on the train and headed through.

At the back of the room was a bay of hovering yellow platforms that fired up into the building. He quickly jumped onto one and began to ascend, whizzing past multiple 'Employee of the Hour' posters, as the platform stopped at various office floors and his fellow workers stepped off.

Despite everything, it looked as if number 46731 might actually be on time for work. Except the man holding the card was not number 46731. The human tied to that number was lying unconscious on the other side of the city. Completely unaware that his identity had been stolen by the man now standing on the platform.

The man called Rogue.

'Oh, 46731, babe, I thought you weren't going to make it,' exclaimed an overly cheerful and chatty Dogkind called Sal, leading Rogue past a row of cubicles. 'You know, you really gotta fill out your paperwork right. Tina in row 78B ended up locked in the crusher down in the sweetening chambers on her first day. Shocking. She was well embarrassed! To be fair, though, if she'd been harvested that'd be the whole supply ruined. Whoosh! Down the plughole.'

They stopped at a small cubicle, and Sal pulled out the chair. 'Well, here you are. First stop, employment!' he chuckled while making the sound of a train. Rogue got the sense that this particular Dogkind regularly chuckled at himself.

'Right, enjoy your home away from home. We have good fun here. Please note we don't do parties on what your kind call birthdays, but you will be required to bring in a cake or whatever your custom is. Bit out of order if not. Allergies are on the noticeboard, don't forget some peeps only eat live food. And the office rules are on your desk. Ta-ra.'

Glad to see the overly cheerful Sal head off, making more train sounds as he disappeared into the bustling office, Rogue sat down. On the desk in front of him were piles of papers with various sticky notes. This included a giant stack of paper that would have taken him multiple years to read, on top of which was printed 'Office rules'. Behind the papers was a tiny, withered plant which was now more twig than alive and an opened can of Gurgle. A note read, 'First can's on us, rest at a discount.'

Rogue watched a tiny fly land on the can, take a big sip of Gurgle then flutter over to the twig plant and immediately die. It was a sad image.

Suddenly, the desk phone rang. Rogue picked it up. 'Good morning, Gurgle—'

There was a crackle of static then a voice said, 'Mailman.'

Rogue nodded. 'I'll just transfer you, sir.' He put down the phone, immediately spotting his target.

There was a spiked and red-faced Zocci in a blue jumpsuit, weaving his way through the cubicles, wearily dropping packages on desks. The wheels of the old mail cart creaked. The expression on the

Zocci's face was pinched and displeased; clearly, he'd rather be in bed.

The Zocci reached Rogue's desk but went past. Rogue leapt up. 'Sorry, I think you have a package for me. 46731?' The alien looked down at the empty cart and back at Rogue, grunted and kept moving.

Oh no.

Panicked, Rogue turned. Maybe there were multiple deliveries, and it had just gone *slightly* wrong. The parcel would get here. It had to.

Then he heard a voice a few cubicles over: 'Oooohh, which one of you sent me a gift? Maybe head office? I knew they'd noticed me.'

Rogue poked his head over his cubicle and saw a man, shaking a parcel. On it was the number '46731', Rogue's number.

He raced over. 'Sorry, sorry. That's mine.'

The man looked back at him blankly. 'But the mailman gave it to me.'

Rogue smiled, trying to keep calm. 'Yeah but that's my number so ...'

He reached out for the parcel, but the man only pulled it tighter to his chest. 'Finders, keepers, mate.'

Rogue bristled. 'But it's not yours. That is—'

'Now, now, what's wrong here?' Sal had returned. He clearly lived for these moments and was going to enjoy this one. 'Look, let's not play the game of "that's mine, that's yours", boys. I mean, who knows? If it's from head office then it could even be for me.'

Exasperated, Rogue shouted, 'That's not from head office!'

Sal growled at him, baring his teeth. Clearly, he did not like being challenged. 'And how do you know that?'

Rogue, exasperated, looked at them both. This wasn't going anywhere, clearly, so he did what he'd almost had to do in the lobby. He reached into his pocket, pulled out a tiny silver disk and threw it on the ground.

There was a sudden rush of air as a small blast emitted, sending a force that pushed both Sal and his colleague back. They landed with a thump on the floor and so did the parcel.

Got you.

Rogue snatched the parcel and with all his might began to run back to the floating platform. He slammed the button for the basement as he heard the sounds of the workers above, yelling for security, coughing amidst the smoke.

As the platform whizzed down, Rogue tore the package open and pulled out what was inside: a blue jumpsuit, an envelope and a small earpiece. He pulled the jumpsuit over his clothes and shoved the earpiece in his ear.

'Well, well, well. I thought maybe you'd decided to leave me for a nice stable career,' a voice joked on the other end.

Rogue smirked. 'Look, Art, you're not getting rid of me that easily. The mailman is clearly not as dedicated to Gurgle as everyone else is here.'

The platform whooshed past more and more offices, as it raced further into the depths of the building.

'Did you get me a can?' Art asked.

'No, you gotta stop drinking this stuff.'

The platform started to slow down, the wall of concrete in front falling away to reveal a large corridor below.

'Oh boo. How is that fair?' Art said, muffled in Rogue's ear.

There was a click as the platform stopped. It had reached the bottom, and Rogue was now standing in a bright pastel yellow tunnel. Both sides twisted into the far distance. On the inner wall were orange steel doors. From behind them came the clanking and thunder of machines, hard at work.

Rogue looked around; it was deserted. 'All right, clear here. How's the tour going?'

The earpiece buzzed: 'Well, your man should be coming up on your left in 5, 4 … no, wait, now. NOW.'

Rogue started to walk slowly to the corner, clutching the envelope in his hand as he heard voices approaching.

'We will next go into Unit Z, Mr Droogle.'

Rogue watched a group emerge round a corner 20 feet down the corridor. At the front was a tall, well-to-do silver humanoid leading a tiny green alien. Hexham Droogle. The founder of Gurgle, in the flesh.

Rogue smiled. *Bingo!*

'Yeah, yeah. Whatever. Just spin me round it once so it's done,' Hexham told his silver friend's kneecap. 'When's lunch?'

Rogue immediately quickened his pace. 'Sir. Mr Droogle, sir.'

The posh alien stopped, annoyed. 'Mailmen are not supposed to be down here,' the alien said.

It didn't matter. Rogue had almost closed the space between them. 'I have a parcel for Mr Droogle,' he said, shoving the envelope at them. 'Please, Mr Droogle, it's important.'

He was barely five feet away; this was going to work when –

BLARN!

The fire alarm went off. Before Rogue could react, the hundreds of steel doors opened and thousands of factory workers piled out. Rogue felt like he was back at the train station again, lost in the sea of Gurgle workers as they all moved in unison back towards the levitating platforms.

Fighting his way through the crowd, Rogue watched Hexham get lost in the throng of employees as the platform he was pulled onto whooshed upward.

When it came to a stop, everyone piled out onto the street. There was a general sense of pandemonium; clearly there weren't many fire drills in this building.

Rogue looked hurriedly through the crowd, desperately trying to spot Hexham again, then the earpiece crackled. 'Shall I come get you?'

Rogue shook his head. 'Just gimme a minute.' He searched through the crowds, pushing past employees who were being assembled into rows by

Gurgle's stressed-out fire marshals yelling, 'Hey, I can't count you if you keep moving!'

Then he saw it, down an alley: a long transport with tinted windows pulling up. That was too nice for workers. Rogue edged towards it cautiously as, sure enough, a large door opened at the back of the building, and out stepped Hexham. This wasn't over yet.

Rogue headed to the alleyway, dodging past the giant rubbish bins and puddles of run-off Gurgle moving quickly towards him when he heard, 'That's him! Right there!'

He turned back. It was his manager Sal, pointing at him. He was with two security guards. Just what Rogue needed. He looked back at Hexham, who was about to get into his car. It was tight, but Rogue reckoned he could make it to Hexham before the guards caught him; he found they tended not to attack when you were holding their boss like a shield.

Rogue broke into a sprint. Hexham heard his footsteps and turned, startled to see this determined mailman approaching at speed. He put his little green hands up, defeated. 'Okay, okay, give me the letter!'

Rogue was in touching distance of Hexham when suddenly a huge force hit him. He felt his feet lift clean off the pavement as he spun in the air a full 180 and slammed down onto the street. It hurt, a lot.

Barely catching his breath, Rogue looked up and watched a shadow casually step over him. Struggling to his feet, he could see, a short distance away, a small reptilian alien. She smiled over at Rogue.

'Oh, hi, stranger.'

Rogue recognised her immediately. 'Morticia.'

She looked down at his jumpsuit and winked. 'Undercover? That's adorable, but why bother with all that when you can just pull a fire alarm?'

Rogue's earpiece crackled: 'She has a point there.'

Rogue watched as Morticia quickly and gracefully launched herself at Hexham. She grabbed him and fastened him to her back, then leapt up onto the nearby office building and began to scale it. Very professional.

There were footsteps behind him, and Rogue realised the security guards that had been set on him were now just a few feet away. His earpiece crackled. 'Tell the tall one to call me once he's vaporised you.'

Rogue grinned. 'Oh, he's all yours.' He threw up his fists and took out both guards with only a few punches. As they fell down unconscious in the alley, Rogue started to run again. He too could be very professional.

'I've been thinking about it, Art, and I'm gonna find a new boyfriend who doesn't choose jobs that are double-booked.' Rogue reached the end of the alley. 'Which way?'

'Take a left then a right – and hey! It's not my fault Hexham is such a desirable bounty. A lot of people will pay a fortune for Gurgle's secret formula.'

Rogue was running through the streets searching the skyline when he saw Morticia racing along the rooftops towards a building that was under construction. Hexham, strapped to her back, was waving his hands in the air and cursing.

Rogue leapt into the control panel of a worksite crane and slammed the levers. The metal basket it was carrying started to creak upwards, full of metal pipes and, after a well-timed run and a jump, Rogue too. The wind whipped through the open-air metal frame as it wobbled skyward, getting stronger the higher he got.

'I'm gonna need you up here, Art…in less than a minute.'

There was an immediate crackle of static and a shout in Rogue's earpiece: 'I can't do that!'

Rogue ignored him, reaching the top of the construction site. Art would find a way. He always did. This was the pattern they tended to stick to: Rogue making slightly reckless death-defying decisions and his poor lovely partner being the actual hero.

Rogue heard footsteps higher up. He took out his blaster and fired it at the scaffolding in front. It came crashing down, and he saw Morticia skid into an uncompleted floor a few levels above.

There was the sound of coughing as Rogue pulled himself up onto the floor. Dust was flying as the wind howled through the sheets at the edge of the room, where a missing wall left a huge drop that went down hundreds of floors into the city below.

Morticia lay in the middle of the unfinished room, spluttering and hissing under her breath. 'Not cool!'

Rogue walked past her. 'Feels pretty fair to me,' he said.

Behind Morticia, Hexham cowered, his hands raised. 'Look, I dunno what you all want but I am sure we can reach an arrangement here.'

Rogue didn't say a word. He had learned it was easier not to try to talk to the bounty too much. Not to get too attached. Just get on with the job and—

A crackle of electricity. He watched as Morticia blinked in surprise then exploded into dust.

Rogue turned. Standing at the edge of the room was a figure in a dark grey cloak holding a golden blaster. Another bounty hunter.

The new arrival moved the blaster to cover him.

Rogue knew full well that he only had moments before he too would be turned to dust. He needed to act fast but there was nowhere to go.

There was a click as a bolt of death fired from the blaster. And Rogue pulled off the kind of coup that made him the exceptional bounty hunter he was. He leapt back with microseconds to spare, scooped up Hexham Droogle and leapt from the tower, sending them both over the edge of the building and flying down towards the city below.

The wind whooshed all around them. Hexham screamed loudly, kicking and struggling. Rogue gripped on to him. 'Just hold on.'

Hexham glared at him, not impressed. Then he bit down on Rogue's hand, drawing blood.

'Owwww! Why? Why?' Rogue cursed, keeping hold of Hexham as they continued to plummet, roughly a hundred feet.

Rogue watched the windows of the tower whip past them and wondered when Art would arrive. Art always did. That was why Rogue loved him; he always came through.

This time, however, the ground below was growing increasingly detailed. Rogue noticed that the red umbrellas on the patio outside the tower had little green stripes on.

Okay, this was getting a bit tight.

Then ... a thump.

Rogue looked down, still clinging on to Hexham. The pair of them were in a large net. Above them, Rogue could see the net was attached to a large steampunk-style ship. They were being pulled in.

Hanging over the edge, doing the pulling up, was a man.

The man who Rogue knew as Art, his person.

Art was tall with shoulder-length curly hair and wore a sleek purple tunic, rolled up at the sleeves. On top of this was a metallic chest-piece that crackled with electrical energy. On his head he wore a pair of steampunk goggles that complemented his striking hazel eyes. As he pulled on the net, a long grey scar could be seen on his arm, a memory from a battle lost years before.

As the net neared the ship, Rogue smiled up apologetically at Art. But judging by the icy look he got back, well – he couldn't smile his way out of this one.

'Why did you jump? I told you I wouldn't make it,' Art said annoyed.

'And yet… here you are.' Rogue smiled, still holding Hexham, who was frankly even more confused now, having fallen a hundred feet only to find himself in the middle of a lovers' spat. 'Should we argue when it's clear I've already won? Why do that to us?'

Art sighed and rolled his eyes, holding out his hand to Rogue and helping him up. Hexham, feeling Rogue's grip loosen, leapt up and immediately ran inside the ship.

The pair of them watched him disappear into the hangar, yelling, 'Help me, these men…'

Art looked back at Rogue, unimpressed. 'Yeah, so, you're dealing with him.'

'Oh, come on,' Rogue called after Art, who was calmly heading back into the ship. Art might act like he hated him, but Rogue knew he wouldn't stay angry for too long. Art always came through.

Chapter 2
An Unwanted Guest

It was 1813 on the planet Earth and a lively party was under way at the Pemberton estate.*

The manor house at its centre was a large, impressive building. The walls were lined with sand-coloured bricks, lit up brilliantly by the perfectly placed lanterns on the lawn. Even the vines on the building appeared to grow in deliberate, organised patterns. Everything about the manor was designed to impress.

The sounds of music and laughter roared from inside; outside, however, there was a sense of stillness. The grounds were large and extravagant. Beautifully designed gardens fell off into the fields and forest that surrounded it.

* To translate, this 19th-century party would be to you, our present-day reader, 'quite a good time actually'. You could also say it would be the kind of party that Ezwoob 9002398 would throw (that's a fun reference for our readers in the 30th century; please don't say we haven't considered you).

It was a balmy night, and a few guests were on the patio, enjoying the fresh air but not daring to stray too far from the party, for fear of causing a scandal. Of course, this did mean the gardens were the perfect place to go if you dreamt of being at the centre of one or were perhaps quite talented with gossip, which Lord Barton was no stranger to.

By Lord Barton's standards, the party so far had been quite dull.

It wasn't that he had expected the Duchess's parties to be anything but a pantomime of the latest fashion and a hot spot for the next big engagement announcement, neither of which interested him. He had wondered if maybe one of the servant girls might rescue the night for him but, right now, he had another, more pressing problem.

A shadow.

'Lord Barton, you are a rake, a cad! You have dishonoured my sister.'

Lord Barton turned to see Lord Galpin. They had known each other since they were boys, and he had been waiting patiently for Lord Galpin to transform into a man worthy of his company. Tragically that day had still not come. Lord Galpin's discontentment was, though, at least something fun for him to play with, until a better alternative arrived.

Lord Barton laughed. 'Galpin, could you remind me to which dishonouring you're referring? Was it the time in the library? The kitchen? The stables?' To be fair, he had genuinely lost track of the number of places he had 'dishonoured' Lord Galpin's sister. He knew for sure that they had never been together in the stables, but then he also knew how Lord Galpin cared for his horse, which would make the idea sting a bit more.

'You will marry her, sir!' Lord Galpin cried, shocked and disgusted.

This was the problem with Galpin, thought Barton; he was so earnest, no fun at all. Furthermore, how could it be his fault that the man's sister had fallen so deeply in love with him?

Lord Barton had always known his looks were powerful, but his peers didn't appreciate the struggle he had. It wasn't easy looking like an Adonis; people often got carried away.

'I will do no such thing, Galpin,' Barton said. 'Now, I am awfully bored of your shouting, and I'm missing quite a good party. So, if you want to challenge me to a duel, then please, sir, do! However…' He took a step towards Lord Galpin, towering over him. 'May I remind you, I am a superior shot. And my friend, is your sister's virtue really worth your life?'

That had done it. Barton waited for the expected feeble apology and swift exit. Then Lord Galpin's expression abruptly changed. He was no longer afraid and looked, bafflingly, impressed.

Lord Galpin smiled. 'Wow. You really are wonderfully bad, aren't you?' He continued towards Lord Barton, thrilled. 'You gamble, have affairs, you're an absolute snake. Meanwhile, I'm all noble and serious.'

The whole demeanour of Lord Galpin was unsettling. He was no longer the fidgety, upright, worried man Lord Barton had been facing before; instead he was suddenly relaxed, confident. He seemed like a completely different person.

'Look at me. I'm soo dull!' Lord Galpin said, flicking the lapels of his jacket, 'Why be this man, when… I'd rather be *you*.'

Before Lord Barton could react, Lord Galpin's hands shot out and grabbed both of his shoulders. His grip was incredibly tight.

Lord Barton struggled and tried to break free, but this was no ordinary fight and Lord Galpin was no ordinary man.

As Galpin's grip tightened, Lord Barton could feel his bones start to push in on themselves and he started to panic.

'Please,' he begged Lord Galpin, but this went unheard. Lord Barton felt Lord Galpin lift him into the air with ease, his silver-buckled shoes trembling above the ground. No one could see or hear goings-on in the garden, a benefit that Lord Barton had always delighted in.

Up until now.

All Lord Barton could see now was the faraway house and the party. Frankly, he wished he'd stayed there.

There was a whoosh of lightning, and blue light enveloped both him and Lord Galpin, accompanied by the sound of twisting and stretching flesh.

It was hard for Lord Barton to see much of what he was up against, as the silhouette of a beaked creature fell over him and a high-pitched caw shrieked into the night. He felt a sudden great pulse of pain in his arms and looked down to see a blue glow passing through his veins.

As Lord Barton felt himself begin to drift away and his body fall to the ground with a thud, his biggest concern was, 'I hope my hair falls right.'

On the grass now lay the corpse of the once legendary Lord Barton, his body drained of life, dried out like a sultana. His eyes were closed but his mouth was wide open, frozen in complete terror.

Then, something peculiar: a familiar silver-buckled shoe stepped over the body. Standing above, instead of Lord Galpin, stood the mirror-image of Lord Barton. He smiled down at the carcass below, brushing down his new 'outfit', pleased.

'Now *I* get to be the bad one...'

Chapter 3
The Party

The last big house party Ruby had been to was for Sarah Petersen's 19th birthday. Everyone took their own drinks, she'd provided snacks, and the decorations were anything they could find on sale at the stationery store – a lot of paper pineapples, chilli pepper fairy lights and a 'Happy 60th' balloon. The music was from a playlist on Sarah's brother's phone, which he wouldn't let anyone else touch. This led to a rival playlist in the upstairs bathroom, which had great acoustics for belting out Dua Lipa.

It had been a good night, all in all, but none of it could have prepared Ruby Sunday for a party like this. This was the kind of party she'd dreamed of.

To suggest the ballroom was grand felt like an understatement. It was huge, and the cornices on the ceiling made the walls look like icing on a wedding cake. Silver candelabras lined the room, giving the cavernous space a gentle glow, and bouquets of flowers tied with ribbons provided a centrepiece at the far end.

There was a separate side room for refreshments. Cloth-covered tables with plates piled with mini sandwiches, biscuits and finger foods. Beside the food was a live string quartet, giving the occasion of eating a tiny sandwich a feeling of extreme elegance.

The guests were all dressed in their finest. As the conversation and dancing flowed about her, Ruby looked around the space, amazed. Tonight, there would be no screaming matches in the kitchen or Sarah Petersen throwing up in her neighbour's recycling bin. Tonight, Ruby was gonna party like it was 1813.

As they walked excitedly to the dancefloor, Ruby squeezed the Doctor's hand, exclaiming under her breath, 'Oh. My. *Bridgerton*.'

He beamed back at her. 'Brilliant, isn't it!'

This time it had been Ruby's turn to choose where they went, and she'd been heavily influenced by her last television binge. She'd always wondered what it would feel like to be in an Austen-style period drama and now she was living the real thing.

Ruby looked at the Doctor and couldn't help but wonder if he had been here before. Was he excited too? Or had he got so used to dropping in and out of time and space that being in the past was no more special to him than getting up in the morning?

And how does he even know when morning is? she thought.

They'd been travelling together for a while now and it wasn't as if she'd seen him have a lie-in, or a day off for that matter. Not that what he did was a job but if there was trouble he had to help, and wherever the Doctor went there always seemed to be trouble.

This evening, the Doctor was the picture of a gentleman, in his burgundy tailed jacket, cream cravat and breeches. It suited him, and he knew it. She looked down at her own yellow Regency dress and white gloves. The look was full-on *Emma*, and she adored it.*

As the music started up once more, the Doctor moved opposite Ruby, giving a deep bow as she curtseyed in response. Neither could stop smiling. *Yeah, he's loving this as much as I am,* she thought.

As the Doctor spun her gleefully around, Ruby noticed she could keep perfect step with the other

* Sure, the TARDIS can travel through space and time, but not enough people appreciate its wardrobe options.

guests. She'd watched the television dances closely, but she'd never pulled shapes like these before.

'How do I know these moves?'

The Doctor gestured at the small pearls on her ears. 'Psychic earrings. Choreography beamed into your motor system. Tap twice to choose your moves, it's like instant *Strictly*!'

Of course he hadn't just given her ordinary jewellery to wear. The first time she'd met him, he'd given her mavity-defying gloves. Not to mention the water-dispersing watch, which had been incredibly useful on the underwater planet of Vespituna but a disaster when washing up at home.

At least these earrings were only giving her the ability to dance.

As they twirled to a stop, the Doctor bowed once more before adding with a hint of concern, 'Just don't set them to battle mode.'

Ruby was keen for further explanation but before she could ask more, they were interrupted by an ostentatious woman rushing towards them, applauding loudly. The Duchess of Pemberton was elegant and opinionated and had the air of someone who owned the place – because, it turned out, she did.

'Marvellous! I thought I knew everyone at my ball, but it appears not,' cooed the Duchess as she admired the Doctor and Ruby.

'Wonderful party, Your Grace,' replied the Doctor with such confidence even Ruby became convinced they'd been invited. How did he do that?

The Duchess couldn't wait to tell her new guests about how well she'd done to create a ball of this standard. 'People are saying a triumph, best of the season, not that I could comment,' she insisted.

'Yes, it was in all the society papers,' the Doctor said. 'Or it will be … I'm sure,' he quickly added.

Then the Duchess's gaze fell on Ruby in a way that made her feel a little too watched. 'But the real estimation of a party is in the matches made, don't you agree, Miss …?'

'Miss … Lady Ruby … Sunday,' Ruby offered, well aware she was still being stared at. 'Of the … Notting Hill estate?'

The Duchess's eyes widened at the mention of an 'estate' while the Doctor stifled a laugh. Ruby hit him playfully on the shoulder.

'And this is the Doctor,' Ruby added, providing the only name her friend ever offered her or anyone else.

The Duchess's face changed from delight to concern. 'A physician as a chaperone? My dear, you aren't unwell?'

Ruby shook her head. 'No, he's just a friend,' she said, looking at the Doctor. Her *best* friend. You couldn't go through the adventures they'd had without forming an extremely tight bond.

The Duchess's face returned to delight. 'A young lady needs suitors, not friends. Come!' With a dramatic swirl, she was off, assuming Ruby would follow.

Ruby turned back to the Doctor, pure glee on her face. 'She's unbelievable and I love her!'

She was about to follow the Duchess when there was a sudden piercing sound from her earrings. She winced. 'Ow, I'm getting feedback.'

The Doctor leaned his head in and rested it against Ruby's as he listened to the earrings. 'Interesting. Sonic interference.'

'Lady Ruby, attend!' the Duchess called, her voice becoming aggravated.

Ruby felt torn. She wanted to follow the Duchess but if something was wrong, she should stay and help.

'Go,' the Doctor said reassuringly, as if he'd read her thoughts. 'I'll handle this. Just try not to get engaged or accidentally invent tarmac; 1902 got away from me. Have fun!' he ordered.

Ruby didn't need to be told twice. 'First one to cause a scandal wins!' she joyfully bet him before rushing off to follow the Duchess.

The Doctor didn't seem worried, so why shouldn't she have a bit of fun? She did hope, though, that he would also make sure to have a fun night. Just one evening where he focused on helping himself, instead of everyone else.

Chapter 4
The Doctor

Rogue was not big on parties. Some might say that this was the choice of someone who struggled to enjoy life, but Rogue's idea of fun was far from the gallivanting Regency spectacle taking place below him, under the balcony.

Watching the wealthy gorge themselves, on wine and each other, he found a bitter taste in his mouth, knowing that far from the walls of this estate, most of the population was living in abject poverty.

Plus, Rogue's idea of a good night out was actually a good night in. Art cooking. Art singing. Chopping. Rogue trying to help but generally being banished and left to disagree with Art about how the soup should be stirred. Now, that was a *real* party.

It was an odd feeling to think nights like that wouldn't be on the cards for Rogue and hadn't been in fact for a long time. It's strange, the shape time takes when you lose someone. One morning they are next to you, on their pillow, and the next morning you realise they haven't been sleeping there for nearly five years.

The five years had gone by slowly and quickly, all at once, Rogue's bounties all blending into one another. It wasn't that Rogue hadn't continued to live, or even to love a little bit. But when you felt you'd lived through the main event of your life, everything else – that extra bit of life you found yourself wandering through – was a bit like an epilogue. Rogue would walk the ship, each night, inspecting every weathered part. A fading heartbeat of a life once lived.

He could no longer think about that day. That time. He felt more ghost than man at this point.

That was why it was so surprising when Rogue gazed down at the ballroom below and suddenly found himself transfixed. There was a man in the middle of the dancefloor. A gorgeous man. But this wasn't just a shallow attraction. There was an energy to the man. An unfiltered joy. Something Rogue instantly knew he wanted to be close to.

Rogue watched as the man twirled his dance

partner around. There was something so freeing and beautiful watching them. It was, as if, in their world, they were the only people on the dancefloor. There was no holding back; this party was theirs.

The dance ended, and Rogue watched as the Duchess immediately interrupted the couple, leading off the man's dance partner. Rogue twitched, seeing the Duchess. It wasn't that he had a strong dislike for her but a feeling of caution that, if he spoke to her, he might find himself accidentally married off and unable to return to his ship or time travel ever again.

Rogue suddenly felt eyes on him. He searched the room and saw that the man, that handsome man, was staring at him. His gorgeous brown eyes beamed up at Rogue from the middle of the crowd. For the first time in a long time, Rogue felt that jolt of electricity when you meet *that* person.

That next person who might be the one to change your life.

Rogue wasn't here for romance, however, or even for a quick stolen kiss in the garden. He had a bounty to catch. He began to look around the rest of the room, pretending he couldn't feel the man's gaze on him. Rogue knew the alien he was looking for could blend in, easily. Being a master of disguise made them an incredibly dangerous target that could be hiding—

'Brooding. Good look. Do you practise in a mirror?'

Rogue turned sharply. The man was up there on the balcony with him. Fast worker.

The man looked at Rogue teasingly. 'Bit more like a frown maybe. Like this?' The man's expression changed. He suddenly looked devastatingly sad.

Not far off my normal resting face, Rogue thought, much to his own annoyance. 'You know, I came up here to be alone,' he said.

Instead of leaving, the man stayed. Confident in his approach. 'Oh, I can see that. Standing there. Good vantage point of the room, watching the exits.' The man stepped closer. 'It's like you're expecting trouble.'

Rogue felt another jolt of that electricity as their arms almost touched.

'You know, I can help you,' the man went on. 'Trouble, I am good at.'

It was then that Rogue emotionally left his body and started panicking a good 50 feet above the scene playing out below. Was the man handsome?

Yes. Was there a bit of chemistry here? Yes. Did the man smell surprisingly nice for someone from 1813? Absolutely.

Rogue, though, was on a mission and what he needed to remember was that the alien he was looking for was incredibly good at playing people. Too good at this dashing stranger game. Would another man make his desires so obvious and open above the bustling dancefloor below? Surely not; it was too risky.

Something was off.

'You planning any trouble?' he asked.

The man winked. 'Oh, honey, I'm just here for the fun!'

'Then go pursue your facile pleasures, and leave me alone.'

The man looked at him, not startled but delighted. 'Okay, rude, Lord ...'

Rogue wanted to smile, it was fun, but he had to keep his cool. 'Not a Lord.'

'Does "not a Lord" have a name?'

'Rogue.'

Immediately, Rogue panicked. It wasn't his actual name – Rogue was the name that Art had given him – but it would do fine. For now.

The man held out his hand to Rogue. 'Nice to meet you, I'm the Doctor.'

'Just the Doctor?'

'Just Rogue?'

Rogue looked at the Doctor intensely. It was clear that the most confident man of the 19th century was not going to leave him alone. This called for a change of plan.

'I need a drink,' he said. 'You coming?'

Rogue could not know yet if the Doctor was his bounty or not, but one thought did go through his mind: *Maybe I do like parties after all.*

Chapter 5
Alice

Alice the housekeeper walked at a pace, trying not to make eye contact with guests as she went.

This wasn't a matter of shyness. She simply understood that locking eyes with a guest would invite conversation and any conversation with a friend of the Duchess would result in a 'small' request (which was never small and never not annoying).

For the last hour, one of these 'small' requests had been to find Daphne, the Duchess's lady-in-waiting. Daphne, she assumed, was probably off with Lord Barton (again), or some other terrible five-foot-nine-sized choice that the young women on her staff continually seemed to make.

Alice felt her shoulders drop as she headed up the grand staircase to the second floor. She had been saving the quiet part of the house for the end of her search. A reward after the loud party below.

Samuel, the butler, passed her. By the expression on his face, she could see he was also counting down the minutes till the carriages left and all that would be heard was the ticking of the clock.

'You seen Her Grace's lady-in-waiting?' Alice asked. 'She was sent for by the Duchess, over an hour ago.'

Samuel smiled warmly at her. 'Probably hiding. Wise girl. I've been told to find a juggler. How?'

They both laughed. She liked Samuel, a lot. Sometimes she fantasised about the Duchess and her merry-go-round of friends perishing suddenly, leaving her to run the manor with Samuel. It would be perfect.

Such fantasies would have to wait, thought Alice, as she continued to the second floor. It was, to Alice's delight, extremely quiet. She walked down a long and dark corridor. The orange glow of the candles lit up the walls, illuminating the garish pictures that the Duchess claimed were art. The rest of the space fell into shadow.

'Daphne?' Alice called, hoping that a door would fly open and Daphne stumble out.

But there was no such response.

Then … a creak from behind her.

Alice turned. No one. 'Daphne, if you've "fallen asleep" in Her Grace's bed again, you will not hear the end of it!'

No response. Alice tsked to herself. There was something wrong with this younger generation, something deeply rotten, she couldn't—

Her thoughts stopped. Dead.

In the shadows, ahead, Alice could see the shape of something. Something almost human.

'Daph?' Alice's voice trembled. The shadow did not respond as it darted back into the darkness. She was alone again. At least, so she thought.

Before Alice could turn around, a bird-like claw grabbed her. She tried to run but it was no use, and she was dragged back into the corridor.

Then it made its call – a piercing, otherworldly bird caw. The party guests below did not hear it, or Alice's screams, over their fun, as the shadow on the second floor feasted.

Chapter 6
Lord Barton

The Duchess kept close to Ruby's side as she walked her slowly about the ballroom, pointing out guests as she went and divulging the known gossip. She gestured to a couple, an awkward gentleman who looked a little sad and an animated lady next to him talking as much with her hands as with her mouth.

'That is Lord Frampton, who earns ten thousand a year! Which almost makes up for his lack of conversation. And Miss Talbot, whom he is courting, and talks enough for the both of them,' the Duchess explained.

'A poor match indeed,' Ruby agreed.

'Never invite them to a dinner party. One needs enough room to walk away,' the Duchess added, as they swiftly passed Miss Talbot.

Next, she pointed out a woman with hair so full of ringlets and flowers it looked like someone had thrown a bowl of potpourri at her and hoped for the best.

'Lady Emerson is rumoured to be with child, which as a married woman would not be remarkable, if not for the fact that her husband has been away at sea for a year!' the Duchess whispered elatedly.

'A complete scandal!' Ruby replied, trying to sound suitably shocked. She was highly amused by the drama of the Duchess's descriptions. No matter how horrified she sounded at her guests, she still invited them into her house for a party. The details of their lives were clearly all part of the entertainment for the evening.

Ruby felt a sudden tug on her arm as the Duchess pulled her round to look at the main attraction. 'Lord Barton!' The Duchess sounded breathless with excitement.

Holding court in the middle of a group of adoring young ladies was a very good-looking man who oozed charm; she could tell at a glance, it just dripped off him. His suit was pressed to within an inch of its life and even the silver buckles of his shoes were shined to a glint.

This was a man who clearly spent a lot of time in front of a mirror.

Despite him having the attention of three ladies already, Ruby saw him look around the room for more interesting prospects. His eyes fell on Ruby and stopped as he gave her a winning smile. Ruby felt herself blush and started to wish she had a fan and maybe a camera.

'Well, that's a tall glass of heartbreak,' said Ruby as Lord Barton extracted himself from his admirers and made a beeline towards her.

'Back straight, eyes bright and smile, if you have the teeth for it,' instructed the Duchess as he approached. 'Many a lady has tried to secure him in marriage, but he is yet to bite.'

As Lord Barton joined them, she daintily held out her hand. He took it and kissed it before looking lasciviously at Ruby.

'Your Grace, where have you been hiding this heavenly delight? An object of such beauty deserves my fullest attention.'

Ruby bristled; Lord Barton was looking at her in the same way as her neighbour's dog, Bingo, looked at a strip of bacon. 'Oh, you're not a tall glass at all. You're half a pint of shandy.'

Disappointingly, this only seemed to spur Lord Barton on. 'I think, my dear, you should learn to be admired in silence.'

'My name's Ruby. Try asking next time you speak to a lady.'

'Fiery. Oh, I like you. A lot.'

Ruby tried not to vomit. 'Well, I prefer a challenge. See ya!' With a small, cheeky wave, Ruby sauntered off, quite pleased with her performance.

Then, behind her, she heard the Duchess chuckle as she rushed over to link arms. 'Lady Ruby,' said the Duchess, 'you might just be my favourite guest!'

Ruby was living her *Bridgerton* fantasy to the max as she continued to 'take a turn about the manor', arm in arm with the Duchess. In fact, she was so caught up with the Duchess's stories it took her a second too long to realise what the grand dame was really up to.

As they wandered, from the ballroom into the grand entrance hall of Pemberton Manor, the Duchess paraded her past groups of suitable gentlemen and wealthy families. Ruby could see them whisper about her as she passed by, wondering who had got the attention of their host.

She was no longer enjoying gossip, she was the subject of it.

'So, Lady Ruby, suitors.' The Duchess squeezed Ruby's arm tighter, no escape, as she pointed out eligible bachelors. 'Perhaps Lord Duthie? Or Lord Alker? His family home is quite extensive and he looks wonderful on a horse.'

'Now that's a Tinder profile,' said Ruby.

'Perhaps talk less when you meet them, dear,' the Duchess said, puzzled but trying to be helpful.

Ruby, however, was already distracted by a large oil painting on the wall.

It was a portrait of a grey-haired woman in a satin dress and shawl, sat posing with her hands placed gently on her lap. Ruby had seen that face before. It belonged to a woman who kept appearing in her and the Doctor's travels, wherever and whenever they went.

'Your Grace, who's that?' she asked, transfixed by the portrait.

The Duchess followed her gaze and frowned. 'The Duke's late mother. Her eyes still follow me around the room. Constant judgement.'

Ruby couldn't understand it. *The woman fits in this time too?* she thought. There was a short cough to her left, and Ruby was dragged away from her reverie by a short, young man with a nervous laugh.

'Hello,' he said before averting his eyes, as if he'd already said too much.

'Lord Alker, this is Lady Ruby Sunday.' The Duchess pushed him closer to Ruby. 'I shall leave the two of you to get more acquainted.'

As she left, the Duchess waggled her eyebrows at Ruby as though she were communicating some master plan, but all Ruby could think was how brilliantly plucked they were and that perhaps she would ask the Duchess later about her approach on this subject too.

Lord Alker and Ruby stood in silence for a few seconds. Lord Alker looked at the floor, the ceiling, the walls and his own punch cup before looking back at her.

'Are you enjoying the party?' Ruby asked, unable to bear the silence any longer.

'Parties are not my favourite,' Lord Alker replied.

No further explanation followed so Ruby pressed on. 'So what *is* your favourite?'

Lord Alker's eyes widened like he had just been asked the most impossible question. He went back to looking around the room, clearly hoping that the answer to what he liked doing might be hidden in the walls somewhere.

'I like cricket,' he eventually remembered.

Ruby knew nothing about cricket but was happy to talk about anything that made the poor man feel more comfortable. 'Oh right, you play cricket or—?'

'No, no, I just watch,' he offered, and the conversation died once more.

So not a love match, thought Ruby.

Lord Alker sipped his punch, with a long slurp, and Ruby's gaze drifted towards a fast-paced young woman, flapping a fan, as she rushed out of the ballroom and into a corridor.

Behind her, Lord Barton followed. 'Emily, please!'

Ruby looked at them. It seemed she wasn't the only one who wanted to run from this man's so-called charms.

Lord Barton caught up to her and grabbed Emily's hand but she pulled away.

'I can't,' she said in a hushed tone.

'Please, a moment, it's not safe to talk here,' Lord Barton insisted as he urged her further down the corridor and through a doorway.

'I also like horses,' Lord Alker announced proudly to Ruby.

Ruby snapped back to face Lord Alker, completely preoccupied by Lord Barton's use of the word 'safe'. She had travelled for long enough with the Doctor to know that if things aren't safe, you deal with them. Plus, she might only have met Lord Barton for a minute, but she didn't trust him for a second.

'So sorry, you must excuse me, I have to, er… check my dowry is intact.' Ruby closed her eyes; yeah, she probably needed to work on her period-appropriate excuses. With a small curtsey, she extracted herself from Lord Alker and pursued the disappearing couple.

Chapter 7
Small Talk

Rogue stared into the crowd, watching the guests laugh and talk to each other. Much to his discontent this room was just as busy as the ballroom, if not more so. He watched the Doctor approach, holding two glasses of punch. Rogue took one and they clinked their glasses together.

'So, have you known the Duchess long?' It was here that Rogue hoped the Doctor was his bounty because his small talk game was not his best quality. Luckily fate stepped in as a blur of blonde hair and yellow petticoat raced past. Rogue recognised her as the woman the Doctor had been spinning joyfully across the dancefloor.

'You okay?' the Doctor said, concerned.

'Yeah. Just, avoiding engagement.' She noticed Rogue. 'So you found a scandal, then?'

The Doctor raised an eyebrow at her as if to say – *you behave!* – but she just laughed and rushed off down a corridor.

Rogue watched it all play out, intrigued. *So his dance partner does know him then. But how well?*

The Doctor turned back and looked into Rogue's eyes, apparently noticing his puzzled expression. 'Don't trouble yourself, love; she won't need me till there's screaming, or smoke, or both. Or Goblins. Right now, I'm all yours.'

Rogue nodded. Okay, Goblins – interesting – but the Doctor could just be a fan of fairytales. This didn't necessarily suggest anything otherworldly about him.

'So, the Duchess …?' Rogue pressed him.

'Oh yeah, the Duchess.' The Doctor just smiled. 'I met her tonight. You?'

Rogue nodded. 'Same.'

The pair of them stood in silence for a moment, then a new voice intruded: 'Oh, Rogue. Come on! He's gorgeous. What you doing?'

Rogue looked over; behind the Doctor, leaning against the staircase, was Art. There was nothing magical going on here. This was merely the fantastical joy of dead boyfriend imagination theatre.

Usually, the imaginary conversations Rogue had with him were when he was alone in the ship but in moments of crisis sometimes, he would imagine him, a life raft in a sea of social interaction nightmares.

'Would you let go, for a second. Flirt back. Ask him about his favourite paintings, the wonders of the universe.'

Rogue looked back at Art. 'He's from 1813.'

Art laughed. 'Okay, well ask him about the wonders of lawn bowls then, who cares.'

Rogue sighed. 'It was always so easy with you. Why can't it be easy with anyone else?'

Art gave him a knowing smile. 'You gotta be willing to let it be easy.' He gestured back to the Doctor. 'Now, come on, you can't just bat your pretty eyes at him.'

Rogue looked at Art and batted his eyes. 'Oh, I absolutely can.'

'What are you blinking at?' the Doctor asked, intrigued, and Rogue found himself snapped out of his daydream and back into reality.

Rogue apologised. 'Sorry. A ghost.'

The Doctor nodded. 'Oh, I know those.' Then, radiating coolness, he took a sip of his drink – and immediately spluttered.

'Thought you could handle trouble?' Rogue grinned. Okay, he wasn't completely dry at this.

The Doctor smiled back, trying to stay composed. 'Now excuse you, this drink was a surprise. A shock!' He continued to sip. 'You know, I think it's kiwi. No, they aren't here for another century. So what are the green bits?'

Immediately, Rogue let go of his fleeting feelings of enjoyment and replaced them with cold resolve. How could the Doctor know something like that? He talked about the present and future like they were all the same to him.

No, Rogue had found his bounty and it was time to get back to work. The manor was too busy, too full of guests. He needed a safer place to capture him. Somewhere he could get him alone.

'Why don't we continue this conversation in the garden?' Rogue said, a flicker of mischievousness in his eyes.

The Doctor laughed. 'Fast mover, let's go.'

Chapter 8
The Dress

Whilst the Duchess was happy that Ruby was getting on with Lord Alker – they'd be engaged by the end of the night, certainly – her mind was distracted.

Earlier, she had spotted Lady Wallace at the party, concerningly in the very dress the Duchess had worn to her last soirée. It was a great embarrassment for Lady Wallace to have made this choice, and the Duchess was determined to make sure that Lady Wallace knew it. To wear something that the Duchess had worn last season was, on the most basic level, incredibly gauche.

The thought did, of course, cross her mind that the dress choice had perhaps been deliberate, a call to war. Occasionally people had dared to cross her, but the idea of Lady Wallace being the one to wield the dagger … Nonsense! Lady Wallace couldn't raise her voice louder than a blade of grass in the wind, let alone make such a bold statement.

The Duchess stepped out of the manor into the lush surrounding gardens – her own design, naturally – where she spotted Lady Wallace on the cobblestoned walkway, deep in conversation. At once, she zeroed in.

'Lady Wallace,' the Duchess said warmly; she always enjoyed playing with her food.

Lady Wallace looked back, flustered. 'Your Grace, it's a beautiful night.'

The Duchess continued, keeping her tone cheery but her words precise. 'Yes. So brave of you to wear that gown this evening, after I wore it so beautifully last season.'

Lady Wallace was of course horrified, and the Duchess knew she had no acting talent. This was genuine remorse. Good. The woman's choice of outfit had been an accident.

Now Lady Wallace was dealt with and there was clearly nothing scandalous happening outside, the Duchess decided to head back to Ruby. Most likely her engagement to Lord Alker would be settled by now, so the night wouldn't be a complete waste of her time.

On her way back to the house, however, something stopped her. Something deeply terrible. Horrific. Monstrous beyond all comprehension... Her housekeeper, Alice – wandering around in the garden, amongst her party guests!

The Duchess marched towards her at pace. 'What on earth are you doing out here?'

Alice turned to face her but not with her usual look of respect and fear for the Duchess. Her face had an expression the Duchess had never seen before.

Alice was unimpressed.

This unsettled the Duchess greatly. Something was deeply wrong here – perhaps Alice had got into the punch bowl?

The Duchess could feel her rage growing. 'I sent you to find my lady-in-waiting an age ago.'

'I did find her. Tried her on for a bit but then I got bored.' Alice sighed. 'I really regret choosing to be staff. It's all work! *You* never let them have any fun.'

The Duchess stared down, puzzled, at the small, old woman. She wasn't entirely sure what kind of joke this was, but staff attempting to jest with their betters was not on. 'Your... language! I'll have you sacked, woman, you'll not sour my evening. People look to me as an arbiter of taste.'

'In that dress?' Alice said, unshaken.

The Duchess wasn't sure whether to scream or slap her housekeeper and was surprised to find she couldn't do either as, suddenly, something was gripping on to her.

Around her mouth was a bird-like claw.

It held on tight and pinned the Duchess to the wall.

Alice leant towards her, her face shifting into that of a monstrous, blue-feathered bird. 'Maybe the dress will look better on me.'

The Duchess felt the hand apply more pressure. She looked pleadingly into Alice's eyes, as many thoughts raced through her head:

Perhaps she should have paid Alice more?

Perhaps she should have gone to church?

Was this dress the right colour to die in?

For a woman of many, many words, the Duchess's final moments were speechless. All that could be heard was a terrible, otherworldly bird-like trill.

It screeched into the night. Ecstatic.

Then a thump, then silence.
The Duchess was dead.

Chapter 9
The Library

The door to the library was slightly ajar, and Ruby slipped quietly inside, quickly heading behind a row of bookcases.

She could hear voices not far away and was ever so careful, placing her feet down softly on the floorboards, not wanting to make a creak, as she moved as close as she could.

When she neared the end of the bookcase, she saw them: Lord Barton and Miss Beckett standing close together beside the crackling fireplace.

Lord Barton looked at Emily compassionately. Ruby was surprised to see a genuine kindness radiating from him.

'Please, Emily, be reasonable,' he said as he took Emily's hand in his. 'Believe what I say.'

'Believe what?' Emily looked back at him unhappily. 'That my sisters were right? You said we wouldn't have to hide.'

And it was here that Ruby regretted following them. She thought she had been chasing danger, but now it felt more like the time she'd got trapped in a toilet cubicle in a Wetherspoon's as a couple broke up outside it.

Lord Barton stared at Emily, imploring. 'And what would you have me do? I rely on the favour of my aunt. She would never approve this match. I would be destitute!'

Emily, close to tears, reached out and touched his arm. 'But you would love me!'

Ruby could feel her heart breaking. This doomed encounter, two hearts in turmoil; it was one thing seeing stories like this on the telly but right now, playing out live in front of her, it hit differently. It took everything in Ruby to stop herself from shouting, 'Just kiss her!' from the back of the room.

Lord Barton took a step away from Emily. 'I am sorry. I will not marry you. Not now. Not ever.'

'Then go! You beast. You stole my heart, leave my reputation.'

There was a pause. Ruby had her gloved hand up to her mouth, hanging on every word.

The air suddenly felt charged as Lord Barton took a step towards Emily, his stare at full intensity, maximum Darcy overload. A stare that must have shattered so many hearts before Miss Beckett's.

Ruby could see why the Duchess warned her about him. This man was lethal.

'And yet … you tempt me still.'

With that, the two of them launched at each other and into a kiss.

A really good one.

Ruby was aware, at this point, she definitely should not be here. If she had been watching this on TV, she would have cheered. In real life, however, she panicked.

Ruby backed away and hit the bookcase, sending a couple of books flying and thumping her on the head. 'Ow, ow, ow!'

Lord Barton and Emily leapt apart, confused by the sounds of coughing and cursing from behind the bookcase. Ruby had no idea how she was going to explain this to the Doctor, let alone to these two.

She peeped out, sheepishly, giving them both a *now you see me* wave.

'Sorry, I didn't mean to, er, interrupt …' Then that horrible silence that can only follow an incredibly awkward moment. Ruby didn't say anything out loud but there was a chorus of suggestions in her head. *Say anything, Ruby. Anything that makes some kind of sense.*

She took a breath and smiled. She had this. 'You two okay?'

Not her finest work but acceptable.

Lord Barton did not look impressed. He headed straight to the door. 'I should not be here,' he announced. 'Good evening.'

The library door pulled shut, and Emily immediately crumpled to the floor, distraught.

'I am ruined!' she cried.

Ruby felt terrible. 'What do you mean, ruined?'

From her pit of despair on the floor, Emily looked up at her, surprised. 'A couple caught alone is a scandal! If the man refuses to marry the lady, she will no longer be acceptable to good society.'

Ruby couldn't help herself. 'Oh, this is so *Bridgerton!*'

Chapter 10
The Night Sky

The Doctor was now walking in the gardens with Rogue beside him, his new favourite brooding stranger.

It was clear that Rogue was hiding something, and the Doctor was determined to find out what that was, even if it meant they had to talk all evening.

Sure, the Doctor couldn't deny, Rogue was incredibly handsome. But there was a greater reason for his locking eyes with Rogue in the first place. When Ruby's earrings had given off a strange signal earlier, he had used the sonic around the ballroom, searching for sonic interference, and this interference, unfortunately, was coming right from Rogue. This meant they both already had one thing in common: neither of them was meant to be here at this ball.

The gardens were nearly deserted so if Rogue was planning anything threatening, the Doctor would soon find out. And if not, well, that was all right too.

As far as settings went for potentially life-threatening situations, he really couldn't have picked a nicer one. They were walking down a long cobblestoned walkway, with hanging vines and little burning torches lighting the way. The smell of sweet peas and roses filled the warm summer air.

The sky above them was rich with stars and, for a moment, the Doctor found himself lost. It was surroundings like this that reminded him why he loved this planet: the nature, the people.

He looked back at Rogue, walking, brooding (of course), and had to remind himself that this was an interrogation, not a date.

'I love these old skies. Ripe with constellations being found and named.' He gestured above, pointing out his favourite constellations. 'The bear, the ram ... the poop-deck.'

'The romance of the night sky,' Rogue replied sardonically as he gave the Doctor an *oh really* look. That stare of his. The Doctor laughed.

'Don't blame me! De Lacaille chose them! Great astronomer, bad with names.' Then he smiled cheekily. 'But if it's romance you're after? He also named those stars there the pump, the chisel and Norma.' Okay, he was flirting now. Ruby would be furious with him if this silly side quest was what got him killed.

'Not what I'm after,' replied Rogue, his tone back to matter-of-fact but his face blushing a little. 'What about you? You've clearly travelled a lot, Doctor.'

'More than you could imagine,' he said, almost tempted to wink. What had got into him?

'I have an idea,' Rogue assured him. He continued to walk at a calm, steady pace. His manner could have been perceived as casual, but the Doctor could see he walked with a purpose. Where exactly was he leading him?

Ahead of them was a large, curved archway of greenery, intertwined with a persistent, creeping flower. You had to admire humans for trying to organise nature into pleasing patterns for enjoyment, when nature disrupted those plans with even more beautiful chaos.

As they entered the narrower section of the path, Rogue stopped for a moment then moved closer to him. The Doctor was suddenly very conscious that their hands were almost touching.

'You *say* you're not after romance,' the Doctor noted, 'and you don't seem a huge party fan. So I have to ask … is that a shoe?'

Sure enough, lying on the path ahead was one solitary slipper. If it had been glass and on the manor steps, it would have felt very *Cinderella*, but instead it lay abandoned in a dark stretch of the gardens.

It felt ominous.

The shoe had a bead-trim and was very fancy. Definitely owned by someone high-class. It had toppled to one side, dust blown around the edges. It must have come off with some force.

The Doctor looked at it curiously. 'No one walks away from a situation with one less shoe. You'd notice. Your foot would get all soggy. You'd go back.' He looked back at Rogue, who nodded. 'Unless it's too dangerous, you're running from something …'

Rogue took a step back, but the Doctor did not see this because ahead he spotted the shoe's sister, just visible, peeking out of a nearby rose bush. He rushed over and moved the hedge back, discovering that the shoe was still being worn, by a very withered foot.

The branches cracked, as the Doctor kept pulling them back until the full nightmare was revealed.

It was a dead body.

At first glance, it would have been hard to tell whose body it was. The skin was now a mottled grey and the face twisted in pain. But the Doctor knew from the carefully styled hair that this was the dear Duchess.

'My poor Duchess, I'm sorry. This is no way to die. In the cold and dark, all alone,' the Doctor said sadly. She wasn't the nicest person he'd ever met but it didn't matter; he wished he could've saved her. No one deserved this. He would not let this happen to anyone else.

Behind his back, he could sense Rogue watching him. His breathing was steady, no words of surprise uttered. It was almost as if Rogue had known she was there. The Doctor turned to face him, certain he had found his villain, and equally certain that Rogue would pay.

'And you knew. You didn't even flinch.' Unsurprisingly to the Doctor, Rogue met his stare, equally confident. There was a coldness to him now, as if a switch had flipped.

'Because it's obvious,' Rogue said, stepping closer to him.

The pair of them were now in a face-off position.

This was beginning to feel like the start of a duel.

Rogue continued to talk. 'This is a murder far beyond the technology of planet Earth. It could only be done by someone brilliant—'

'And monstrous,' accused the Doctor.

'And ruthless,' snapped Rogue.

'And contemptible,' the Doctor shouted.

Neither moved an inch. Neither would back down.

'YOU!' they both shouted.

There was a momentary pause then they both began to talk again...

'You,' they both said.

Another pause.

'No, you!' again in unison. This clearly wasn't going the way either of them expected.

The Doctor waved his hands, determined to stop this ridiculous situation. 'Excuse me, I think you'll find—'

'You!' concluded Rogue as he whipped out an ornately styled steel-and-copper blaster from his jacket and pointed it right at the Doctor.

Well, the Doctor thought. *That's one way to win an argument.*

Chapter 11
The Wallflower

Miss Emily Beckett was the middle child of three sisters. The Duchess had described her to more than one acquaintance as, 'Bookish and vapid, I fear. But good teeth.'

Emily loved reading and sewing and had notable skill on the piano, but suffered from nerves when playing in front of an audience. She was known for being polite, if a little quiet, and she always ate in a measured way, so that any onlooker would find her dainty. In short, Emily was a model member of early 19th-century society. But that did nothing to help her marriage prospects.

What she lacked was a family with money.

Marianne, her elder sister, had married respectably, but her husband did not have enough to provide for the family. When Emily's father's health declined, there was considerable pressure for her to marry above her station. So it was obvious that this was not the time to fall in love with a lord who had no intention of marrying.

Emily had known Lord Barton for two years now. Their paths had crossed at many events, and every time there'd been this frisson of excitement. He was a risk-taker who got a thrill out of living on the edge of what was or wasn't allowed when out in society. Emily found this thrilling and completely different to her own nature.

When a party was due, she took her preparation incredibly seriously. Sitting for hours in front of her mother's mirror, she would practise the right things to say or do. She longed to be perfect. When she met Lord Barton, she longed to be perfect for him.

The pair of them had first met at the races. The crowd in all their finery were placing bets. Chance had led Emily to be seated next to Lord Barton in place of a sick cousin.. Though she would never have wished smallpox on anyone, this infection had led to the greatest evening in Emily's life.

Lord Barton had dismissed her immediately, challenging Emily on her knowledge of the event.

Much to his surprise, however, she had taken him to task. She had given him a detailed account not only of the competitors' names but also of their odds. She had always loved racing. They had spent the entire evening side by side, only parting when the sun rose.

Later, others told Emily how wonderful they had looked together, and this simply solidified her belief that they could all see what she had felt: a true connection of love.

At the next party, however, Lord Barton had acted like he did not know Emily at all, and it had crushed her. How could their evening together have mattered so much to her and not at all to him?

A pattern was born. The pair of them would circle each other at events, stealing moments together whenever they could. Stolen kisses and promises in the empty rooms of various extravagant manor parties. When Lord Barton was with her, he made her feel that she was his world, but when they were apart it was as if he forgot she existed; his focus was on his family duties or on making his own fun.

Tonight wasn't any different. At this particular party, Emily had found herself alone in the library with Lord Barton. He was, yet again, full of promises of love but none of marriage.

Every romance novel that she read had convinced her that true love would always find a way. So why did she always feel stuck in the chapter of heartbreak? Ending every encounter disappointed, crying and alone.

Well, not alone.

Not tonight.

Through her tears, Emily looked up at the young woman who had interrupted them in the library. This stranger hadn't instantly run off to tell everyone the scandal she'd witnessed, but no doubt she would, any second now.

It would be the talk of society: Emily's shame and her secret love.

To her surprise, however, the lady in the yellow dress sat down next to her. Her face had an odd look, one she hadn't seen from her peers before. A look of kindness. When the lady handed her a handkerchief, Emily started sobbing into it.

'I knew his reputation. I had only hoped... Oh, I'm a fool.' Emily blew loudly into the handkerchief. It felt good to talk to someone.

'You aren't a fool for having hope. If you ask me, *he's* the fool,' the young woman said. 'Among other choice words.'

This attitude surprised Emily; that a woman should so happily insult Lord Barton, a man of such considerable status and fine looks.

The young lady then gave her name simply as 'Ruby'. Emily replied with her full name because she had been raised to follow etiquette.

'Please don't think harshly of him,' Emily said, picking up her fan and waving it in front of her face, frantically, a nervous habit she couldn't help. 'His station in life is too tenuous, he must find a good match. And I have no dowry to speak of.'

'Sounds like he's choosing his cushy lifestyle over love,' Ruby surmised.

'Cushy?' Emily said, excited to hear a new word. Then she saw Ruby frown, as if the woman had made some sort of social faux pas.

'Um, it means comfortable, like a cushion,' Ruby said awkwardly.

'Cushy,' Emily repeated, thrilled with the new vocabulary. 'I like it!'

'Yeah, okay, maybe don't use it a lot,' Ruby added swiftly.

'Yeeeaaah, okay!' Emily let the new words roll off her tongue with joy. 'Your words amuse me. You aren't like others here. You seem different.'

There was a look from Ruby, a flicker of guilt. Emily wondered what she was hiding. Perhaps she was secretly in love with a lord too?

'I'm from a very progressive town,' Ruby said, squirming slightly as Emily watched her. She was pretty and her tone had this mix of being both gentle and tough. She looked no more than 19 but was clearly worldly far beyond her age. Perhaps she had travelled continents? Whatever her reasons, Emily was grateful; she knew she could instantly trust Ruby and her judgement.

'Well, thank you, Miss Ruby. Most people here would delight in the gossip, not offer me comfort,' Emily confided.

'Yeah, well, my mum always says, if it's not your life, why you telling it?' Ruby smiled fondly. 'She's annoyingly smart.'

Emily found herself wishing her own family gave her such kind words or warm memories.

'Anyway, your secret is safe with me,' Ruby told her.

The words were delivered with such sincerity that Emily knew them to be true. She felt seen and safe. Then her new confidante rose and held out her hand.

'Right. You know how I forget about a guy?' That frown again as she corrected herself. 'A gentleman, I mean ...' Ruby broke into a smile. 'I go dancing!'

Emily closed her fan and put her hand in Ruby's, ready to leave this room and sorrow behind her. She was no longer crying alone at a party.

Miss Emily Beckett had made a friend.

Chapter 12
The Stranger

As far as bad days went, this wasn't the Doctor's worst.

The gardens were beautiful and he hadn't been incinerated yet by that fancy-looking blaster. He hadn't seen a blaster like that before, which, for him, was incredibly exciting as he had seen most things.

Rogue was, however, firmly pointing said blaster at his back.

The Doctor tried to reason with him. 'You know this isn't a good look for you. In any century.'

'Keep moving,' Rogue replied languidly. Another day at the office for this guy.

The Doctor turned his head back to check on the glowing chamber of the blaster. 'Is that a glo-stick?'

He knew he had said something good because he got the biggest reaction from Rogue yet, hearing him grunt then look immediately offended.

'Glo-stick? I made this!' Rogue bit back.

Okay, we have an ego here and apparently an inventor, thought the Doctor. *That's—*

'Cute,' he said, which only spurred on Rogue.

'It's not cute, it's a disseminator. It's *very* complicated.'

'Like its owner.' The Doctor grinned. He figured if he was going to get killed, he might as well enjoy himself.

Rogue just looked at him, annoyed. His pace was dropping, which meant that wherever Rogue was leading him, they couldn't be far away.

'So, who do you think I am?' the Doctor asked.

'I *know* you're a Chuldur.'

The Doctor felt a thrill of excitement. 'The shapeshifters!' he exclaimed, excited to pull at this new thread. This made his night *very* interesting. 'I mean, I've heard of them but never met one…' He looked at Rogue playfully. 'Unless I have?'

'Adorable, but you can drop the act. The Chuldur travel planet to planet and try on people like outfits, all for the fun of it. You can't trust a word they say.'

The Doctor raised an eyebrow; this was pretty rich coming from a man who'd lured him into a garden and drawn a weapon but okay, fine. Sure. You do you, babe.

Rogue's expression remained focused. 'It's nothing personal, Doc. I've been paid good money to find you.'

'Okay, firstly, "Doc"? No thank you, sir, please. And secondly...' The Doctor stopped walking and turned to face Rogue. Only the disseminator between them both now.

'You're a bounty hunter? That is ... so cool.' The Doctor could see by Rogue's expression he wasn't used to his captives being so joyous. 'Catching monsters, getting into scrapes.' He looked deep into Rogue's eyes and stayed there a moment too long. 'Meeting handsome strangers.'

Rogue was fighting not to smile back. 'I'm here for the money, nothing more.'

'So where are you taking me?'

'My ship.'

'Yeah? And where'd you hide a spaceship in 1813?'

The only thing in front of them was a forest clearing. Unless Rogue was travelling the galaxy in an acorn (which was some aliens' vehicle of choice), there was only one explanation.

'It's cloaked. Past that shed.'

The Doctor turned back to see what 'shed' Rogue could be referring to and was horrified to see it was the TARDIS, nestled further down, amongst the trees. Okay, to be fair, he probably shouldn't have been so honest about the disseminator because this did sting a bit.

'Shed?! That's *my* ship.'

'You travel in a shed?'

The Doctor knew Rogue was mocking him a bit, and to be honest he didn't mind at all. 'Love the shed.'

'Why isn't it cloaked?' Rogue asked confidently.

'It's behind a tree!' As far as captures went, this had now definitely become one of the strangest.

Rogue pulled a device out of his pocket and clicked it. There was an almighty whoosh and a change in the air as a second ship started to materialise. It was large, and built from all kinds of metal. A patchwork of different metal ship parts to make a new Frankenstein creation. Across its bow was written the name *Yossarian*.

Rogue looked at the Doctor cockily. 'Now, *that's* a ship.'

Chapter 13
Shaking it Off

Thank goodness for psychic earrings, thought Ruby. She dipped, swung and danced about the room with grace and poise, moving arm to arm with each passing gentleman. She felt like the queen of the ballroom.

Ruby and Emily had danced at least five dances in a row. Ruby watched now as Emily spoke to a captain in a long red coat and tails. He bowed low before offering his hand. Emily would forget about terrible Lord Barton in no time, Ruby was sure of it.

As the soldier led Emily to the dancefloor, Ruby caught her eye and gave her a thumbs-up. Emily raised a thumb in response, with a confused look on her face. Well, when did the thumbs-up start anyway? It could be now.

Ruby was proud of herself. She'd helped a shy wallflower realise the thing that makes you the belle of the ball isn't your status, outfit or dowry. It's all about confidence. Ruby curtseyed to her new partner, the reticent Lord Alker. The man may have been bad at conversation but that didn't mean he couldn't dance. She strongly believed you can't judge a person by your first impression.

Everyone has bad days.

The music began to play. It was a quadrille, which was danced in sets of four. To Lord Alker's delight, Ruby grabbed his hand and pulled him towards her new friend Emily and her uniformed dance partner.

However, someone else moved, at pace, onto the dancefloor and blocked their path. It was Lord Barton. He gave Ruby a smug little nod as he and his dance partner joined their four.

The dance started in earnest, and the four interlocked hands as they circled, left then right. Lord Barton was staring at Ruby with an intensity she didn't like. Couldn't the man stare at the person he was dancing with?

Confidence was one thing but Lord Barton had ego for days.

Yes, Ruby had definitely met people like him before. The type of person who was used to being fawned over because they have good looks, money or, in the case of Ryan Fletcher, a car. The kind of people who are spoiled by life: they get what they want with minimal effort so they never really learn to try.

Admittedly, Ryan Fletcher wasn't that bad. Ruby had gone out with him for two months until she realised he cared more about the car than actually going places in it. When she had broken up with him, he had looked so surprised, like it would never occur to him that someone wouldn't want to be with him.

Lord Barton, meanwhile, looked like there was something else under his charming surface. If he didn't get what he wanted, he wouldn't be surprised. He would be angry.

The couples split and danced in their pairs. Ruby was relieved to be opposite the placid face of Lord Alker. Then her feet moved again, controlled by the pace of the earrings, and she was spun into the arms of Lord Barton. Of course, this had to be a dance where they swapped partners. Ruby silently cursed the earrings for not being able to warn her of that.

Lord Barton looked a little too pleased to get her alone. 'Ah, the book fan. Hope you weren't too shocked by anything you saw in the library this evening?' he said as he pressed his hand on Ruby's back, holding her close.

He was surprisingly strong; he wasn't applying much pressure, but she could feel she wasn't able to back away.

Instead, she leaned in, ensuring that their conversation was private. 'So am I right? That if a man and woman are caught alone together, they can be forced to marry?'

'My, my, are you threatening me?'

'No,' she said, playing innocent. 'I'm just glad it's only me who saw. Emily can do so much better.'

'Excuse me?'

There was the anger. This guy was too easy to rile and Ruby enjoyed doing it. People like Emily walked in this century so men like him could run, and Ruby had lost her patience. It was about time Lord Barton learnt that not everything would go his way. It was also time that he loosened his grip.

She twisted free and patted him on the shoulder. 'Don't hang out in a library unless you wanna get read.'

With that, she walked off the floor mid-dance, leaving him stranded and partnerless.

There were some murmurs from guests around the floor as they spotted Lord Barton standing straight as a pole and alone in a sea of moving dancers. There was no hiding the fury on his face as he marched off, embarrassed.

As the dance finished, Emily rushed over to Ruby, her face flushed with excitement. 'I can't believe you did that.'

Ruby shrugged. 'I can't believe you like him.' She looked around, but there was no sign of the Doctor. Or the Duchess, thankfully.

Emily looked over at Lord Barton then back to Ruby. She opened her fan to hide her massive smile and leaned in close to her. 'Best party. Ever!'

Chapter 14
The Yossarian

You can tell a lot about a person by the ship they fly in, thought the Doctor. *It's home away from home.*

Which explained why he was shaken by what he saw.

Granted, he had made some assumptions about Rogue, but this dimly lit and cluttered space was not what he had expected. It was an absolute mishmash of tech, half-made projects, tools and strange-looking things in piles or cages. It looked and smelt like a mechanic's workshop.

In the corner was a cockpit for flying, pretty much hidden behind a stack of metal toolboxes and a hammock slung in the corner, he assumed for sleeping but perhaps eating as well?

Oh, Rogue, he thought. *What happened, love?*

'So,' he said. 'This place is a mess.'

Rogue did not engage, walking over to the console on the other side of the room. The disseminator was still in his hand and pointing right at the Doctor. It glowed a brilliant bright orange, ready to blast.

The Doctor tried to ignore this and focus on the *Yossarian*. The mess aside, the make of the ship did not surprise him. It was an old asteroid hawk from the 50-56, often sold on the cheap in many star systems. If anyone's ship was a shed, this was the one. He looked across the console, trying to see if there might be anything useful to help him escape or at the very least steer the conversation towards suggesting Rogue should get a broom.

On the console was an Ood translation sphere, plugged into the ship's controls. It would allow Rogue to understand the local languages wherever he travelled, but the Doctor's attention was taken more by the can of unfinished Gurgle balanced dangerously on top. It was a dusty can. Left there a long time ago.

'Rogue, honey, you need company.'

'I live alone,' Rogue replied coldly.

'Baby, I can see,' said the Doctor. 'But that wasn't always the case, was it?'

His question caught Rogue off-guard. That little pause of breath; for a moment, the tough dangerous bounty hunter exterior was gone.

Rogue approached the Doctor. 'Why do you ask?' he said, setting down a metal box on the large hexagonal workbench next to them. Tools were scattered across its surface.

'This an old asteroid hopper, piloted by two.'

'Well, not any more,' Rogue said. He opened the metal box in front of him, took out a silver object and snapped it effortlessly into three even pieces. Rogue grabbed the Doctor's arm and moved him with ease to the middle of the small metal pieces. 'Stand there.'

The bounty hunter's strong, the Doctor thought. *Confirmed.* He looked down at the small triangular pieces of metal surrounding him. 'What do those things do?'

Rogue looked at him smugly. 'It's a trap. Triform on!' He gave a little *ta-da* motion as the floor around the Doctor's feet turned jet-black. From one piece, a brilliant glowing white light zoomed to the next, and the next, then on to the first, connecting all three. The final result was the outline of a white-glowing triangle.

The Doctor tried to move his feet but found it was no use – they were firmly stuck to the ground, held there by an incredibly strong magnetic pull.

'Oh, I see. My name's Bond. Molecular Bond,' the Doctor said as he watched Rogue walk back to the workbench. 'And you think I can't do anything, standing still?'

'It also works as a Transport Gate,' Rogue said, not even looking at the Doctor, keeping his eyes on the console.

'Yeah, well then.' The Doctor reached into his pocket and pulled out his sonic screwdriver, raising it proudly up and exclaiming, 'Triform off!'

He wiggled his feet. Nothing.

Uh-oh.

Rogue looked at him like, *Was something supposed to happen then?*

The Doctor just shrugged with a *Yes, I meant that to happen* attitude and said, 'My gadget can do more things than your gadget.'

'You're not scaring me,' Rogue said. 'The ship would have registered whatever *that* is' – he gestured rudely to the sonic – 'as a dangerous device.' He typed gleefully into the console. There was a ping. 'And instead it says… screwdriver.'

He paused. 'Which is convenient as I've been wanting some new shelves over there.'

The Doctor looked back at him sarcastically. 'Oh, ha ha. And no, but it does do all sorts of things.' He lifted the sonic up to his eye, trying to search the ship for a way to win back some power in this conversation. There had to be something in here he could use against this man, or at least to his own advantage. As he looked through the screwdriver, it magnified the distant surfaces of Rogue's ship, scanning for information, anything helpful.

Then he came across something he had not expected to see. Hidden amongst some tools were some orange dice, all placed inside a metal tray. The Doctor could see the dice were D20, D12, D10, D8, D6, D4 and a percentage dice. The Doctor laughed to himself. He had once spent a long weekend playing D&D with the Paternoster Gang (Strax had played a bard with a surprisingly beautiful singing voice).

'Did you get your name from Dungeons & Dragons?' asked the Doctor.

Rogue flashed a quick smile. 'Roll for insight.'

There it was! Some warmth finally. The Doctor hoped there'd be more; he didn't fancy being sent off to wherever Rogue's bounties went and having to negotiate with someone else. 'Oh, I'm sorry, was that a wee smile from the most serious man in history? And it says that you are wired for sound ...'

The Doctor clicked the sonic, eager to hear what would play, expecting a lute or something similar but ...

Kylie Minogue started to blare loudly around the ship, and not just any Kylie, classic Kylie. The fine dining choice from her music menu, 'Can't Get You Out of My Head'.*

'Now, this is a surprise,' the Doctor cried. 'Love this! Classic.'

He watched Rogue run over, horrified, as he frantically hit buttons on the nearby console, anything to turn off the banging pop anthem.

'So, do you play this before missions to get in the zone, or—'

The music stopped. Silence returned to the cockpit.

The Doctor shrugged and pressed the sonic again; there was another whirr as Kylie began to play in the room once more. He was still stuck in his triangle of doom, but this didn't mean he couldn't dance.

Rogue ran back to the console and clumsily hit more buttons, but this time the music wouldn't stop.

---

* It is, of course, destined to become Earth's national anthem in 4055.

He paced over to the Doctor, who was now miming the lyrics, and tried to grab the sonic off him.

'Too slow… close… miss again… At least try!' the Doctor mocked as he moved the sonic out of Rogue's reach. 'I'm just standing still, baby.'

Finally, Rogue snatched the sonic from the Doctor's hands and turned the music off, clearly rattled. 'Have your fun, Doctor. You've got very little time left.' Rogue gestured down to the trap below.

'Oh, right, yes, death, peril,' the Doctor grumbled. 'So, where it is you are sending me? To your employer? Or…' He looked hopeful. 'On a holiday?'

'To an incinerator,' Rogue explained matter-of-factly.

The Doctor felt a chill down his spine. 'It's a death sentence?' He had assumed Rogue had come here to capture a Chuldur, not destroy it.

'You're a killer,' Rogue replied, with no remorse. His expression had returned to the cold-hearted determination of a man on a mission.

The Doctor could see by Rogue's change in demeanour that he should probably have spent less time dancing and a little more time escaping.

He needed to get out of here. Fast.

'I can't turn it off till it's charged, and once it's charged...' Rogue picked up a long silver cylinder, with a switch on the end, a trigger. 'I press send.'

The fun was definitely over.

Chapter 15
A New Outfit

Lord Barton sulked in the corner of the ballroom, clutching a glass of wine. He was unaccustomed to sulking at one of these events and did not want to make it a habit.

As a Chuldur, he travelled to play about with the lives of others, not to be toyed with himself.

Tonight, he had deliberately chosen to be the bad guy so he could dash hearts and be adored. Then that Ruby girl had ruined it!

No, he did not like this. He did not like this at all.

Still, it didn't mean his entire evening should be spoiled. He could change outfits. Find a new path to go on. Perhaps he could become someone bumbling again?

'Having fun, darling?'

Lord Barton looked up to find the Duchess approaching, glass of wine in hand, looking thrilled with herself. In the brief time he had known the Duchess, he had never known her not to be. Her gloating was the last thing he needed: salt poured in his wounds by the world's most annoying hostess.

That said, if he wanted to be someone new, the person in charge wouldn't be a bad choice.

Of course, he would need an excuse to get her alone but how fortunate she would count herself, to be a part of Lord Barton's roster of stolen kisses, surely? He didn't feel up to seduction right now, but perhaps he could waylay her with some urgent delicate matter… something about a missing glove, perhaps?

But as she drew closer, something about her smile seemed suddenly far too familiar.

'Do you like my new outfit?' She struck a dramatic pose.

Of course. He knew the smile of another Chuldur. 'You're the Duchess? I wanted to be her next.'

'Too slow, love. Although I hoped someone here would be royal. Clearly the Duchess doesn't know *everyone*.'

Lord Barton drank from his glass of wine. The Duchess and he had travelled together for nearly a decade now. She was the one who planned these excursions and, like the woman whose form she wore, she had impeccable taste when it came to creating the perfect party.

'Do you think it's too much for the wedding?' The Duchess looked down at her new body, clearly looking for compliments.

He was about to answer when he heard a familiar laugh across the room: Ruby. She was on the other side of the ballroom, being asked to dance, yet again. His eyes followed her as she waltzed across the ballroom. Even her dancing irritated him. It was precise, effortless. But he knew how to take the perfect revenge on the seemingly perfect woman.

'I can think of a better outfit for you to wear,' he said, a malicious grin on his face.

The Duchess followed his gaze.

'Lady Ruby Sunday.'

Chapter 16
The Artificer

The Doctor was starting to get frustrated. 'Rogue, I am telling you, you have the wrong man. I can prove it.' He reached into his pocket and pulled out his psychic paper in its leather holder. 'This authenticates me as non-Chuldur.'

Rogue approached, curiously, to take the paper. The Doctor knew he would soon be out of this mess. The paper would psychically link with whoever laid eyes on it and tell them what he needed them to hear.

Rogue looked at the paper, grinning. 'It says, "You're hot."'

'Does it?' the Doctor replied, flummoxed. 'I'm sorry. No.' He hurriedly grabbed the wallet again and slapped the paper. 'It's broken.'

'Is it that I'm hot or you're hot?' Rogue leaned in. 'Who is hot, Doctor?'

'It means the temperature!'

'Suits you, flustered,' Rogue said confidently. 'It's a good look. You should try it more often.'

'Says the man trying to kill me,' said the Doctor, unimpressed.

'Gotta do my job,' Rogue said. 'But as it's been so nice talking, I'll check for the paperwork…' He trailed off as he walked to another part of the room and began typing. 'This job is all paperwork ever since we got that new Boss. File this and categorise that. A real yawn-fest.' Rogue looked back up, that cheeky handsome grin again.

Suddenly, there was a beep followed by a beam of light. It moved across the room, straight for the Doctor.

As it hit his face, the Doctor felt a slight warmth off it. He heard the ship say, 'Scanning,' then he saw one of his old faces appear, the one he had before this, projected next to his. His bi-generation friend.

This Doctor liked that Doctor, and hoped he was getting to relax all those miles and years away right now. Not a care in the world. His only worry being what biscuit next to dunk in his cup of tea.

'Well, the scan confirms it.' Rogue gave a *told-you-so* scoff. 'Shapeshifter.'

The Doctor sighed, shaking his head.

'*Transport Gate fully charged,*' the trap declared. '*Press send in ten vexils.*' The Doctor's one-way trip to the incinerator was coming up fast.

'How long does a vexil last?' the Doctor inquired.

The trap immediately answered his question. '*Nine…*'

Rogue leant against the counter and picked up the trigger.

'*Eight…*'

'Nice knowing ya, Doc.'

The absolute outrage of it! 'Rogue, wait!' The Doctor spoke quickly. 'I'm telling you, you've got the wrong man—'

'*Seven…*'

'And if you kill me, you leave a Chuldur out there on 19th-century Earth! Think of all the innocent people who will die.'

Rogue just shook his head.

'*Six…*'

'You still have a choice. Your hand is on that trigger.' The Doctor looked at him. 'Can you really take a life when there's a chance you could be wrong?'

'*Five*…'

'Okay. Fine! Well, if I only have five vexils, then I beg of you—'

'*Four*…'

The Doctor once again pulled his psychic paper from his pocket, but this time he launched it into the air. It soared across the room.

'*Three*…'

'Look!' The paper hit the scanner, which pinged into life.

'*Two*…'

The Doctor did not dare to break eye contact with Rogue, whose finger still hovered over the trigger button.

'*One*…'

He closed his eyes, bracing himself for a horrifying fiery death, but then… nothing happened. He opened his eyes again. Rogue was still holding the trigger but was transfixed by something. He was looking at the scan next to the Doctor.

The scanner had continued from where it was before, but this time it had moved on from the Doctor's last face and was showing more. Different past selves of the Doctor, different genders and ages, all projected on top of his current form. Right now, standing in the middle of the *Yossarian*, he was revealing his true heart. His power. His strength. His undeniable wonder.

The Doctor looked from the scan back at Rogue, right in the eye. 'I am not a Chuldur. I am something much older and far more powerful. I am a Lord of Time from the lost and fallen planet of Gallifrey.' He took a deep breath. 'Now, let me go, Bounty Hunter. We have work to do.'

Rogue just stared in awe, taking in the Doctor, all of them.

'You're beautiful,' he said.

Years before he dragged the Doctor onto the *Yossarian*, Rogue was sitting at the console with Art.

There was a romantic dinner in front of them, the console acting as a makeshift dinner table. In the middle, a large pot bubbled and steamed as the pair of them ate from two small bowls, opposite each other.

'You are so stubborn!' Art said, lowering his spoon. 'I told you not to put more chilli powder in, yet here we are.'

Rogue laughed. 'Look, I tried really hard to make us this terrible meal.'

'Now, hold the phone, I did not say this was terrible, I just said you deliberately ignored my advice.'

'Unwanted advice,' Rogue replied. As he took another mouthful, a tear started to form in his eye. The stew *was* too hot, but he was never going to let Art know that.

'I can see you crying,' Art said. 'There's a literal tear, rolling down your face.'

Rogue looked at him, faux dramatic. 'I'm just feeling really emotional about my chair over there, that you still haven't fixed.'

Art laughed. 'Oh, it's your chair now, is it?'

Rogue smiled and wiped away the tear he had pretended was not there with his sleeve. He continued to look around the ship, at the home he and Art had made together.

. Art had had built everything on the *Yossarian* and nearly every gadget Rogue used on the missions. The emphasis on 'nearly' was because Rogue had foolishly attempted to build a few of his own. It was a learning curve for him. A steep one.

Where Rogue had charm in spades, Art had a talent for turning a kitchen spoon into a deadly laser ray. He could do anything.

The name Art had also come from Dungeons & Dragons, a shared pastime and passion between them both. Art was short for Artificer; this was a class in the game known for their invention and incredible ability to see the full potential in objects, and it suited Art to a tee.

Rogue could never pin down exactly when the nicknames had started. Like so many things when you've been with someone for a very long time, it had begun as a cute reference, but then the nicknames just became everyday for them until, eventually, the old names just didn't fit any more. They were just Rogue and Art to each other. And that suited them both just fine.

'You know, I could go undercover next time,' Art said, taking a sip from the can of Gurgle, by his food.

Rogue hated that stuff so much, but Art loved it; he could make a comment about it but, he figured, let the man enjoy his drink. 'Oh yeah,' Rogue said playfully. 'Last time we tried that, you gave someone our actual contact details.'

'We got on! An alias shouldn't prevent an actual friendship.'

Rogue nodded.

He got up, went round the console and put his arms around Art, nuzzling into his shoulder. 'I guess it's how I met you,' he said, and the pair of them laughed.

Art smelt like a warm fire. He was taller than Rogue, only by a bit, but it meant he looked up to him slightly, which was a bit of a novelty for Rogue, who was usually the tallest in the room. He took in Art's face: every line, pore, the stubble, the striking, hazel eyes. Art looked back down at Rogue, and it looked as if he was about to say something deeply profound or romantic.

'So, is this your apology for dinner?'

Rogue leant in closer. 'Oh, never,' he murmured.

The moment would have been quite sweet if there hadn't been a grunt, from the other side of the room.

The pair broke apart, forgetting that they were not alone. Not quite yet. Rogue looked over. Tied up in the corner of the room was Hexham Droogle. The founder of the Gurgle drinks company. Their meal ticket.

Art looked at Rogue. 'Do you think we should feed him?'

Rogue shook his head. 'Nah,' he said. 'He bites.'

Rogue could not have known this would be their last week together. This was the inescapable. They could jump through time together, see so many beautiful worlds blossom with life and watch that happen over and over, but this did not mean that either of them could escape time themselves.

In some ways it was time's greatest gift, the not knowing.

Back in 1813, Rogue was walking towards the blue box with the Doctor, deep in that exact thought. He wondered how long he would have with this new and wonderful stranger, and then also why he was troubling himself with the thought at all. He could feel an excitement building in his stomach; it was terrifying, all the ways in which this could go sideways.

The Doctor stopped, a few steps ahead. 'You ready for this, Rogue?'

It was funny hearing someone else call him that, but his name sounded good being said by the Doctor. Rogue liked it. It fitted.

'It's not my first shed,' he replied. He walked up to the blue box, pushed open the door and took the first steps into the next chapter of his life.

Chapter 17
Impolite Society

In the grand entrance hall, Emily was thrilled to be huddled together with Ruby, her new favourite friend. She had now danced seven dances at the Pemberton ball. Seven! And not one with the same gentleman. Her sisters must be wondering what had come over their usually more reticent sibling. Miss Ruby had provided her quite the inspiration. As for Lord Barton, she hadn't thought of him in nearly thirty minutes.

'I thought I ran about a lot with the Doctor, but that was just exercise,' exclaimed Ruby as she poured them both punch. 'Good thing the music's stopped for a bit.'

The entrance hall was busy, and Emily searched for Lord Barton, hoping she might spot him spotting her, having fun without him. She wondered how he was feeling; he had barely looked her way since leaving the library. Perhaps he had seen her dancing and was now off somewhere feeling incredibly jealous. Yes, that was what was happening. He was no doubt regretting the way he'd abandoned her without a proposal; perhaps at this very second he was plotting ways to win her back.

Emily, of course, could not accept an offer of marriage from him now. Her time with Ruby had made her realise that she was more than capable of making her own fun at a party, with or without his attention. Even if he once again professed his love, how could she entrust her heart to a man who had thrown it aside so willingly? It would take no end of promises, gifts and attention for her to even consider him again; something that would prove not only to Emily but to all society that she was worthy of his complete adoration. Only then could a proper and fitting marriage proposal be accepted.

Emily glanced over at the doorway to the ballroom, waiting to see if an admonished Lord Barton would emerge. Instead, she saw the Duchess.

The Duchess waved. 'Cooeee! Lady Ruby!'

Ruby ducked her head down and groaned. It was an actual groan with no attempt to cover her mouth.

It's as if she's a stable boy! thought Emily.

'She wants to marry me off,' Ruby said airily. 'I shouldn't have danced with Lord Alker.'

The Duchess pushed past her guests (and their compliments), making a beeline for the pair. Emily recognised the look of determination on the Duchess's face. But the Duchess didn't even glance in her direction.

Her focus was solely on Ruby.

Usually, Emily would never stand in the way of a host's wishes yet, as she watched the Duchess advance and Ruby's face contort into a grimace, she made a choice that surprised herself. She grabbed Ruby's hand and gave it a brief squeeze.

'She'll have to catch you first!' Emily's usually coy face was full of mischief as she pulled Ruby away, towards the staircase.

'Are we even allowed up here?'

'Not in good society. So we had better not get caught!'

Emily and Ruby laughed as they raced up the stairs.

* * *

Ruby felt quite proud of Emily. She'd known there had to be a little rebel underneath all that fan waving; she'd just had to find it.

They had briefly paused at the top of the staircase, to see the Duchess down below, circling in confusion, having lost them in the crowd. As she started to raise her head to look up higher, the two dived round the corner and out of sight, still laughing.

Upstairs, the house was as fine as the rooms below. The corridor stretched out in front of them, lined with wallpaper of florets and crowns. Cabinets and tables sat on either side decorated with ornate vases, trinket boxes and candle holders.

It reminded Ruby of an antiques fair her mum had taken her to. She half expected the items to have price tags on them, which her mum had assured her were merely a starting cost that you haggled down from.

Emily walked ahead, looking at the paintings on the wall. 'I can't believe I did that!' She seemed jittery and excitable. 'I just couldn't bear the thought of losing you to the Duchess.'

'Don't think I could bear it either,' joked Ruby. She'd had enough of the Duchess for one evening.

She wondered if the Doctor was having as much fun as she was.

Ruby noticed a door, further down the corridor. It was open a crack. She gestured towards it, and Emily gave an excited nod.

They pushed open the door and wandered into a large, unlit bedroom complete with a four-poster bed, fancy dressing table and huge wardrobe. From the small amount of moonlight through the window, Ruby could spot an array of make-up and brushes laid out on the dresser.

They had entered the master suite, the Duchess's bedroom.

Ruby and Emily gave each other a little grin. Emily sat on the edge of the bed as Ruby cracked open the wardrobe. Ruby ran a hand over the long dresses contained within. By the textures she could feel, each was decorated extensively with lace, satin or jewels, and whatever was at the far end of the wardrobe felt like feathers.

Emily leaned back on the bed with a comfy sigh and spread her arms out on the blankets, like she was making a duvet angel. 'I never normally make friends at these things,' she confided, her voice suddenly sad and sincere. 'Even my own family avoid me; they think I'm boring. But with you, I'm really having fun.'

'Me too,' said Ruby and she pulled out a long pink dress from the wardrobe, the one that was covered in feathers. She held it up to herself. 'Is this too much?'

Emily laughed and shook her head. 'If anything, it's too little!'

Ruby threw the dress over a chair and sat down next to Emily. 'You're not boring.' She softly nudged Emily's elbow. 'You're the most interesting person I've met here.'

Emily shrugged, clearly not convinced. 'You'll think I'm silly but I'll spend hours before a party practising what to say. I have to be perfect.'

'Perfect is impossible. I aim for good enough.'

Emily gave her a curious look. 'Don't you care what people think of you?'

Ruby gave this some thought.

Her mum was always caring for her, for others. Her house was busy with life and love. It was also loud. She'd adopted Ruby, but there were many others she'd fostered before and since. All of them were encouraged to say what they thought, provided they also listened to each other. So, when out and about, Ruby had a habit of saying exactly what was on her mind. Never mean, but always ready to argue for what was right and listen for when she was wrong.

'I'm always me; people either like that or they don't,' Ruby concluded. 'And that way, I find friends that like me for who I really am.'

Emily looked wistful as she nodded, taking that in.

Ruby got up off the bed and offered a hand to pull Emily up. Then she caught sight of something that startled her.

There was a dark figure under the bed.

'Emily,' Ruby whispered, motioning her to rise.

Emily got up cautiously and the pair of them lifted the blanket, slowly. They both gasped as they realised the figure under the bed was dressed in a maid's uniform. It didn't look to be breathing.

As Ruby crouched beside the body to check for signs of life, Emily gripped her hand, unintentionally tugging her backwards. The body rolled over, the maid's face now staring right up at them.

It was warped and gnarled. Her eyes were wide open, sunken and set with fear.

Ruby leapt back, shaken.

She knew straight away that this was no ordinary death. This was otherworldly, strange.

This was something the Doctor needed to see.

Then Emily fainted.

Chapter 18
Inside the TARDIS

Rogue walked through the blue door into an impossibly giant space. It was much bigger on the inside, the best magic trick he had ever seen.

Except he knew, of course, that this wasn't magic.

Rogue had met many dreamers and magicians in his travels. It was surprising how many had bounties on their heads; he immediately recalled quite a complicated winter with Houdini. But this was no mere shadow play of smoke and mirrors. It was beyond the magnificence of any ship he had ever known.

The ceiling curved upwards in a white dome-like shape, with lights dotted evenly on every wall, glowing as they rippled with colour. The curve in the space did not make the room feel any smaller however; it was at least, Rogue thought, forty metres from himself to the furthest wall.

In front of him was a large and long walkway that snaked around the room. A white railing ran alongside it and, on its surface, Rogue could see grey markings along every curve it took. He raced along it, joyful, seeing it wind down towards the centre of the room, where a large console dominated the space.

The console was covered in bright blue and red buttons, surrounded by gears and controls Rogue could not even comprehend, let alone recognise. At its top were glowing tubes that reached out from the centre, like a powerful tree trunk, fading off into the brilliant white finish as it met the ceiling.

It was clear that this ship, like the *Yossarian*, had lived a lot of lives, thought Rogue; there were so many memories within its brilliant clean walls. But the main thing that impressed him was how stylish it all was. How well placed and how welcoming. Rogue had only known the Doctor for one night, but it was clear this ship was perfectly made for the person who travelled in it.

'I'm in love!' Rogue exclaimed. The Doctor raised an eyebrow at him, so Rogue gestured around. 'With this machine,' he added quickly. 'Dimensionally transcendental.' He teasingly dusted his hand along the white railing in front of him. 'And so clean!'

'Yes, the things you don't recognise are *surfaces*,' the Doctor teased, standing by the console. 'Now, trap, please.'

Rogue handed it over but immediately regretted doing this so willingly. Sure, this man's ship was brilliant. But the trap, that was his.

The TARDIS made a loud groan.

Rogue frowned. 'What was that?'

'Nothing. Just indigestion,' the Doctor said, giving the TARDIS a little comforting tap. 'She gets upset by bounty hunters. The moral void. No offence.'

Rogue rolled his eyes – *Yeah, yeah* – and the Doctor held out his hand again.

'And your disseminator?'

'Only if you handle it carefully,' said Rogue, keeping his eyes locked on the Doctor, worried what the plan could be for his precious creation.

The Doctor took it calmly. Then he snapped the disseminator in half.

'Hey!' Rogue shouted.

'Do you want to save everyone or not? Look, watch me.'

And Rogue did, as the Doctor moved some parts from the disseminator into Rogue's trap, then attached it to the TARDIS, using cables. Rogue found himself fighting not to remember the hours of work that building the disseminator had taken. He had to let this go.

'Okay, pass me the hyperdyne link,' said the Doctor. 'Blue wire, under the switch, there.'

Rogue did as he was told, eager to see exactly what new monstrosity the Doctor had turned his favourite gadget into.

The Doctor grabbed the cable and plugged it into the newly upgraded trap. It sizzled slightly.

'I can't believe you broke my stuff!' Rogue complained.

The Doctor stopped what he was doing and looked at him, dead serious. 'Whatever the Chuldur have done, I can't let you kill them. I also can't let them kill others. So, instead, we'll send them to a random, barren dimension. No one to hurt there and no way back.'

'Random? So I can't trace them,' Rogue protested.

The Doctor just nodded as the trap continued to whirr behind them. 'Don't pout too much. When we're not trying to kill each other, we're a good team.'

Rogue smiled begrudgingly. 'So, this ship is from the ancient and fallen world of Gallifrey, you say. Where is that?'

'Well, I might take you one day,' the Doctor replied. Then he drummed his hands on the worktop, pleased. 'All right, in a few minutes that will no longer be a death trap. You're welcome.' He turned to look at Rogue and his expression was curious. 'Who did you lose?'

'What?' Rogue said, trying to keep calm.

'You lost someone.'

'How d'you know that?'

'Because I know.'

Rogue thought for a moment, conflicted. 'There was ...' He paused, feeling Art's face in the back of his mind, the horrible echoes of that final day. 'Yeah.'

He looked back at the Doctor. His expression wasn't judgemental; it was the face of someone really listening, with not just bargain-bin sympathy but real understanding. Like, he got it.

Finally, Rogue felt the words tumble out of him, the words he'd been needing to tell someone for the last five years. 'We travelled together. We had fun. You know.' He took a breath. 'And then a day came along and at the end of that day ... I lost him.'

He sighed, that great pain in his chest.

'What about you?'

'I lost everyone,' said the Doctor simply.

'But the party...' A million thoughts were running through Rogue's mind. 'I saw you with that woman?'

The Doctor just looked back and smiled. 'My best friend.'

There was a pause, and Rogue stopped himself for a moment, not wanting to ask the question he so desperately wanted answered. He shuffled nervously. He had to know. 'Do you ever wonder... Do you ever wonder why we keep going?'

'Because we have to.' The Doctor put his hand on Rogue's arm. 'We have to live every day because they can't.' Self-consciously, he turned and gestured around the TARDIS. 'You know, you don't have to stay a bounty hunter. You could travel with me. Oh, the worlds I could show you, Rogue.'

'And what if I like what I do?' Rogue got the feeling that when people met the Doctor, they would often uproot everything for him.

Why should that always be the case? Rogue had just as much to offer in adventure.

'Would you travel with me?'

'That is quite an argument.' The Doctor nodded. 'Tell you what, when we both get out of this, let's argue across the stars.'

'I'd like that.' Rogue felt that swell in his chest, that nervous energy as he took another step towards him. He was very aware that their faces were almost touching. It would only take one of them to lean a bit closer, and they were already so close, so close that they could almost—

Ping! The console in the TARDIS chimed.

'The trap is ready,' the Doctor said, and the moment was gone. He moved back to the console as Rogue stood there, recovering. He could hear the Doctor speaking down at the console, but he barely registered what he was saying. He just nodded, lost. What was he getting himself into?

Chapter 19
A Letter to Rogue

Dear Rogue

It feels silly, writing you this letter, but I hope it finds you. So we're clear too, I don't want this to be interpreted as a Please don't mourn for me *or some other such nonsense. Honestly, I am quite irritated that it wasn't you that died...*

Would I say that? I suppose.

Whatever helps your imagination.

I know you've likely dreamt up and read this letter many times.

I fully understand why; I was good chat. However, if only for your negotiation skills, I hope you've made at least one friend since my passing.

Imaginary letters from dead boyfriends can't be your only form of communication.

Of course, if the person reading this is his only friend then I gleefully warn you: Rogue is stubborn.

He says he will clean that particular corner of the ship, but I promise you he won't. I spent ten years asking and I could have put that time into something actually productive. I could have learned at least five more languages in the time I would have saved.

So take my advice. Give in to this reality. Admit defeat. It will never happen.

A few other things to note: his snoring can and will wake up the most dangerous animals, and for some reason – despite eating pretty much everything – bread with any kind of seeds or olives in is an absolute no. I agree, it's a real failing on his part.

Apart from this, however, what you will find is a great man who I loved with every part of my soul. Please give him a hug from me and do not name a child or dog in my memory when you move in together. A cactus is fine, though.

And Rogue, if it is you reading this letter, don't let me worry about you. I did enough of that when I was around and oh, the time I wasted.

Don't hide.

And please don't go fixing up our ship for ever. I was the mechanic anyway.

Live. Talk with everyone. Laugh. Dare to ask someone, 'Is this seat taken?'

And, most importantly, don't forget to dance. That's the best part.

Yours,
Art

Chapter 20
The Dance

The Doctor walked quickly back into the bustling entrance hall, Rogue at his side.

He had only one thought on his mind, now: to find Ruby.

He hated to interrupt her night. He knew that she had been really looking forward to this party. But he needed to know she was safe and nowhere near the Duchess.

Then he saw her. Racing down the stairs with a startled Regency woman behind her.

The Doctor ran towards them.

'Doctor!' Ruby said. She looked as relieved to see him as he was to see her.

They began to talk over each other.

'Ruby, there's an alien shapeshifter—'

'Doctor, there's a body upstairs, someone or something—'

'—disguised as the Duchess.'

'—killed the housekeeper.'

'Oh, you know,' they concluded together, taking a pause from their tennis match of words.

'Killed?' said the Regency woman, becoming even more agitated.

The Doctor looked at her sympathetically. He could see how tightly she was gripping on to Ruby, as if afraid she might fall off this Earth if she let go.

'Hi, I'm the Doctor. What's your name?' He always found introductions not only polite but also a useful distraction from fear, and he could see that this poor woman was terrified.

'Miss Emily Beckett,' she said with a curtsey, her hands still trembling.

'She's my friend,' Ruby said, giving the Doctor a look that could only be read as, *Be gentle, she's been through a lot*. He understood. Any new friend of Ruby's was automatically a friend of his.

'Don't worry, Emily, I can handle our … intruder,' he said kindly.

Emily looked comforted for a moment, but then even more confused.

'Should we be telling humans?' Rogue asked cautiously, leaning in behind him.

The Doctor noticed Ruby's curious expression. 'Oh! Ruby 2024 and Emily 1813, this is Rogue, he's a bounty hunter and almost incinerated me.'

'A mistake he said he was letting go of.' Rogue held out his hand to Ruby and Emily, who both went for it at the same time and ended up shaking it together.

'We've had quite the evening,' the Doctor said.

Ruby raised her eyebrow and smiled knowingly. 'Oh, I can see that.'

'But what does it all mean?' Emily gasped. 'Are we all going to die?'

The Doctor and Ruby exchanged a look: *Who is going to take this?*

To their surprise, Rogue stepped up.

'There's a creature from another planet at this party,' he said. 'Highly dangerous, it can look like anyone it's killed and if it gets you…' He looked at her, dead serious. 'It'll drain your life in a second.'

Emily's eyes widened and she hurriedly began to fan herself, presumably as an alternative to fainting.

'We need to work on your people skills,' the Doctor said as Ruby put her arm around Emily, trying to calm her. 'Now, let's find our Duchess!' He looked over at Rogue, exhilarated. This was one hell of a first date.

Couples danced in the ballroom as the string quartet continued to play. On the edges of the room, groups watched each other. Some were eager to make matches, and some eager simply to enjoy the delicious canapés passing by on trays held by smiling servants.

The Doctor, Ruby, Emily and Rogue made a third group.

They were all staring at the Duchess, who was on the other side of the room, speaking with Lord Barton.

'We've got to get her on her own. She won't attack in the open,' Rogue said, watching the Duchess hiss at a guest passing her, like an angry goose.

The Doctor smiled; this had given him an idea. He looked at the others, excited. 'Oh, my goodness, it's cosplay!'

Rogue looked at him, baffled, not seeing how that could possibly relate.

'Rogue, no, really, look, you said they come to a planet, try on people like outfits, all for the fun of it! Think about it,' he said, happily. 'They're cosplaying.'

'Wait, so it's literally dressing up and playing *Bridgerton*?' Ruby said, getting it. 'They're doing what we are, well minus the death and all that.'

'Yes!' The Doctor nodded enthusiastically. 'Those TV signals beam across the stars. Why not?'

'What are these tee vee signals?' Emily said curiously.

'No time.' The Doctor looked at her, apologetically. 'And look, if we need to get our Duchess alone, we all know there's one thing that attracts her.' He smiled. 'Scandal, outrage and –' he looked right at Rogue – 'plot twists.'

'She wants the most exciting role to play,' Rogue realised, watching the couples on the dancefloor bow as the song ended.

'Exactly,' the Doctor said as he turned to Ruby. 'You and Emily stay in here, keep people inside. As long as you and the guests aren't alone, you'll be safe.'

'Like Lord Barton?' said Emily, happy to turn the conversation back to him. Ruby gave the Doctor a *just don't ask* look.

'Sure, protect Lord Barton,' the Doctor said. Hearing the next dance beginning, he turned to Rogue and held out his hand. 'We'll be bait.'

Rogue smirked. 'I don't see how us dancing will create a scene.'

'Then you should have researched this era more, because *we* –' he looked intensely at Rogue, very much enjoying himself – 'are scandalous.'

Rogue grinned and took the Doctor's hand. The pair went out, right into the middle of the dancefloor. This was going to be fun.

The couples around them were following a simple routine, rotating in pairs. But the Doctor and Rogue entirely ignored this, doing their own thing. The quartet were inspired, shifting their music into a more intense piece.

The Doctor could already feel people starting to turn and whisper but his focus wasn't on that.

All he was thinking about was Rogue.

Rogue's hand on his shoulder, his chest. Rogue's eyes locked with his as the pair of them turned and twirled across the floor.

As the pair of them continued to move gracefully across the floor, pressing their bodies close in perfect synchronicity, a crowd had formed on the edges.

They turned towards a group of women and the Doctor overheard one exclaim, 'Oh, my, ladies, this is shocking,' and he was pleased, but this wasn't enough. He could see the Duchess had snapped her fan closed and her attention was on them, but she'd need something juicier to follow them outside.

'We need to have a big fight so I can storm off alone and draw her to us,' the Doctor said, spinning Rogue away from him.

'Can't I storm off alone?' said Rogue. 'I would rather not talk in front of this many people.'

'Oh, come on, Rogue,' said the Doctor. 'I'm sure you talk to lots of people. Your bounties for a start.' He gave his hand a little squeeze and whispered, 'I believe in you.'

'Doctor, please!' Rogue protested.

He was too late.

The Doctor pulled away from him and gasped. 'How dare you, my Lord!' he shouted. He was incredibly pleased to hear the music stop immediately, the crowd turning to stare. It was so deliciously dramatic. 'You would ask me to give up my title, my fortune –' he chewed up every word, really hamming it up – 'but what future can you promise me?'

Rogue didn't say a word back. He just looked at him pleadingly and stuttered slightly.

'Say anything,' the Doctor whispered, then raised his voice again. 'Tell me what your heart wants, or I shall turn my back on you for ever.' By way of illustration, he literally did turn his back on Rogue. He looked at the crowd, hearing nothing but silence behind him.

Then a gasp.

The Doctor turned and faced Rogue again, who was now down on one knee. He had pulled off a ring from his finger and was holding it up to him.

Rogue was proposing. Fast mover indeed.

The Doctor knew this was a moment of fun, for the drama. Despite that, he couldn't stop a jolt of panic.

'Sorry ... I can't,' the Doctor said. He raced out of the ballroom, and Rogue chased after him.

Chapter 21
Back in the Garden

Rogue ran out of the manor and into the gardens, looking for the Doctor. It was much quieter outside now all the guests were inside. He looked up at the night sky. He was pretty sure he spotted the 'Norma' constellation.

The worlds I could show you. That's what the Doctor had said to him in the TARDIS. A phrase that was playing over and over in his head.

There was a whistle ahead.

Rogue looked over and saw the Doctor, waiting for him, hidden behind a hedge. He felt a rush of excitement as he tried to focus.

He'd not been asking the Doctor for marriage, but for some simple commitment. A sign he should stay longer than this one adventure.

To see those worlds he'd promised. At least for a little while. Now he couldn't stop wondering how much of their connection was real and how much had been for show.

'Quite the show,' Rogue said with a sly grin.

'You did pretty well yourself,' the Doctor replied, adjusting his collar.

As they waited, Rogue felt their shoulders lightly touching. It was funny to think that the last time they were in this garden, he'd believed the Doctor was a monster he had to catch.

Now he was trusting him with his life.

Rogue peered from behind the hedge. The Duchess ought to be here any minute.

'Remember, we've got to keep the Duchess talking,' he said. 'A Chuldur is strong and if she starts to change you, she won't stop.'

The Doctor nodded, wide-eyed with concern. 'Quick question. How many does the trap hold?'

'One.'

The Doctor's gaze was still fixed on the patio ahead. Rogue stepped out from behind the hedge to see what he was seeing.

On the patio stood the proud figure of the Duchess. She wasn't alone.

Next to her stood Lord Barton, Miss Talbot and Lord Frampton and to the back – was that a butler? They were no longer chatting like Regency socialites but instead watching the Doctor and Rogue intently.

Like predators.

There was a burst of blue energy as the Duchess's face transformed from that of a human into one that was bird-like. It was feathered and full of excitement: her true Chuldur form. Her yellow eyes glowed in the dark of the garden.

'I want to be the Doctor. Who wants to fight for the other one?'

'Me, me, me!' the other Chuldur greedily yelled, licking their lips as they too morphed from people into horrible bird-creatures. Their Regency clothes remained but their new faces were contorted, twisted, shaking with alien shrieks of excitement. They were ready for the hunt.

Rogue looked back to the Doctor as he realised what they were up against. 'It's a whole Chuldur family.' He grabbed the Doctor's hand and shouted, 'RUN!'

'I'm usually the one who says that...' the Doctor said as Rogue wrenched him away.

The pair of them raced, hand in hand, deeper into the garden. The sound of Chuldur laughter grew closer behind them.

'Gentlemen, we just want some fun!' they heard the Duchess yell as they entered a courtyard. The walls in here were high, covered with flowers and hedges, boxing them in, nowhere to go.

Rogue changed direction again, frantically looking for an exit, when—

'BOO!' Miss Talbot leapt out at them. Her happy sing-song voice called to the others: 'I've found them!'

The Doctor dragged Rogue sharply right and down through another cobbled archway. They saw the other Chuldur in the distance ahead, searching amongst the topiary.

Miss Talbot remained on their tail: 'This way! This way!'

Rogue only dared look back for a second, but he could see the Chuldur racing towards them with glee, the Duchess leading the charge. 'I want to be the Doctor. Breaking spines, removing tonsils, live vivisection!'

The Doctor and Rogue headed down another walkway, covered in vines. One entrance, one exit.

'Find them!' the Duchess snarled at the other Chuldur. 'I want a new look!'

The sound of the Chuldur's footsteps seemed everywhere about them now. They continued down the walkway, running with all their might until they exited into an open field, a large pond a few feet in front of them. It shimmered in the moonlight.

Rogue looked left to right. No trees, no hedges, no cover. They heard squawks of excitement from the walkway behind them.

The Chuldur were catching up.

Rogue's eyes were desperate as he looked at the Doctor. 'We have about five seconds till they're on us.'

The Doctor gave him a confident smile. 'Long enough.' With that, he led Rogue straight towards the pond.

The pair of them dived in.

There was a sharp piercing feeling as the ice-cold water hit Rogue's chest, his lungs. He held his breath.

On the surface, they could see the rippling images of the Duchess and some of the other Chuldur moving about nearby. What they were saying carried only as mutters through the water, but Rogue could see the Duchess's arms gesticulating bossily to the others, as their shadows rushed past, still looking for them.

Taking his eyes off her, Rogue looked down, wondering how deep the pond went. Beneath him, the water was shadowy, but something glinted silver in the weeds below.

He dropped down further, realising he was looking at a silver cufflink on the sleeve of a body. Horrified, he tried to kick back up again, to push away, but his foot got caught in the weeds.

The body loosened in the commotion and the husk floated closer. It was Lord Barton. His sunken eyes stared up at Rogue while his Chuldur copy searched the grounds above.

Rogue was panicked, losing air. He wanted to move and cry out but the shadows of the Chuldur still danced across the surface of the water. He had to swim up, now.

Then he felt the Doctor's hand take his, gripping it in comfort, steadying him. Telling him he wasn't alone down here. Rogue held on and stayed beneath the water until the shadows left. Then together, they swam up.

The breath when they hit the surface was like

the best meal Rogue had ever tasted. He drank it in, inhaling deeply as the Doctor checked the gardens ahead. They were finally alone.

On the banks of the pond, the pair of them dragged themselves out. Rogue's shirt was stuck to his body; the Doctor's was the same. They were both drenched through.

They looked at each other and laughed.

'Okay, Ruby was right, this is a bit Mr Darcy.' The Doctor wrung out his jacket as Rogue shook the water from his boots. 'Is the trap working?'

Rogue reached into his pocket and turned it on. It glowed for a second then fizzled out. 'Nope.' He threw it over to the Doctor so he could check it himself.

'We may need another plan,' the Doctor said, inspecting the trap.

Rogue pondered this, looking at the landscape. They had run through most of the estate grounds and the manor was now small in the distance. Safely far away. The Chuldur now a problem on the horizon.

Rogue agreed that they would need a new plan, and he knew exactly what they had to do.

'We need to leave,' he said.

Chapter 22
A Short History of the Chuldur

Some readers, less familiar with intergalactic travel, may not be as aware of the Chuldur as others. I'm looking at those of you who have only met species from your own planet. You may think you're well travelled because you've been on a different continent, but in the scheme of the universe that's as impressive as rolling over in bed. To get us all on the same page, here is a short history of everything we* know about the Chuldur.

There are very few accounts of the Chuldur recorded in intergalactic historical records. Or, to be more accurate, there are very few *known* accounts. This is the incredible thing about Chuldur: they can look and act like anyone that they have killed.

* By 'we', we mean those of us who have travelled at least as far as the next solar system over and found the nearest corner shop. There's always a corner shop.

Taking their memories, mannerisms and extensive garden gnome collections (or whatever it is you prize so dearly). This means, theoretically, *any* account of *anyone* could be a Chuldur and we would never know. Makes you wonder why we keep records at all.

What we do know about the Chuldur is as follows.

The Chuldur in their original form are feathered, beaked and winged creatures, roughly the size of a humanoid. Once they're in their new form, there is no way to tell them apart from the being they have become. They hide in plain sight and can perfectly mimic your colleague, friend or loved one for as long as they wish. They can switch between their original form and their taken form at will, keeping as much or as little of the taken form as they like.

The times they are in Chuldur form are your only hope of detecting one. However, they are usually only in this form when they are about to kill again.

There are other, smaller indications that one of these Chuldur has taken over the life of someone close to you. Look for changes in behaviour in those you know well.

You may find yourself arguing with a family member over nothing, or having a charged conversation with a superior who has changed their mind on a project at the last minute. You might find yourself swept up in a love affair with someone you barely know or having a shouting match in the street about how a spacecraft is parked. If your peaceful life suddenly feels infused with needless drama, then you are likely in the presence of a Chuldur.

The Chuldur's home planet is rumoured to be in the Scymerion region. It has a surface that can change in colour and appearance, meaning it looks like a continuation of the stars around it. It can only be spotted by observing the gravitational impact on the objects in the planet's vicinity.

Beyond their planet, there are only occasional records of a Chuldur presence being discovered. By nature, they are as varied as any other species in the known universes, but they appear to have one thing in common: a desire not to be found.

The Chuldur were first rumoured to be involved in the business of espionage during the Time War (the dates of which are continually changing). They were known for selling information to the highest bidder by infiltrating spaces and places others cannot.

With the reputation of their skill growing, many factions were known to search for their home planet to employ them. Those that returned were often suspected of being Chuldur themselves.

The only known images of Chuldur in their true form are by renowned AI painter B3X7G in his art piece 'The Purists'. This painting now hangs in the Current Art Gallery and depicts a small group of Chuldur society who have sworn that they will take no form but their original bird-like one as a matter of principle.

For the persistent researcher, there are a couple of clues as to how the Chuldur have travelled to and impacted other planets.

For example, one record* tells of a Chuldur order that has vowed only to take the forms of dying beings.

These Chuldur give comfort to loved ones to help them through the grieving process and then honour their new form by travelling in it for a year, completing acts left undone in their chosen victims' lifetimes. There are references in wills and estates from a number of planetary areas indicating that a Chuldur shall continue in the deceased's form in order to honour their legacy. (Although in many

* Shadow Proclamation footnote SPZ9-110866701

instances this practice was later discovered to be an inheritance tax fraud.)

Their ability to infiltrate societies became more widespread, which led to a rise in what became known as the 'Chuldur defence', often asserted in legal proceedings. There are PR statements about embarrassing family members or criminal associates, attesting they were in fact Chuldur at the time of their terrible behaviour. Many people found it preferable to claim they were duped by a shapeshifter rather than admit to being friends with, or related to, someone awful.

A more recent example of Chuldur activity has been that attributed to the Partrian family, a group of thrill-seeking Chuldur known for treating the forms they take as nothing more than outfits to wear. They travel from planet to planet as if shopping for a new look and take lives as if they were toys to play with. The Partrian family were said to have visited the Royal Palace of Majenka and the once famous Raleepian racecourse. However, there are no confirmed accounts of their presence as neither place had any survivors.

The only verified account was of their visit to the City of Capriskia in the Debraskan quadrant.

The first odd occurrence involved the local judiciary suddenly acting in a capricious manner and creating new rules based on their latest whims. Tributes were demanded whenever staff were entering or leaving a judge's chambers. Scandals became commonplace amongst the court officials the same day. A wave of gossip and rumour spread throughout the Capriskian legal system, then, very suddenly, all went quiet. The doors of the courts were locked and the hallways of justice fell silent.

It took a week before they found bodies in the river, lifeless and drained, as if they had been dead for months. There was confusion and anger, as each subject found had been seen alive and well only recently. There were rumours of an invisible beast, hunting people at night, and talk of families turning on each other, friends fighting in the streets and the occasional whisper of 'They look like us'. The citizens of Capriskia were advised to remain in their living quarters until further notice for their own safety, but this didn't help. The Chuldur had infiltrated the city and wanted to continue their games. Only when the Chuldur grew bored did they reveal their true faces and ensure there were no witnesses left. Apart from one.

Professor Sarsha Melenney remained locked in her office at Capriskia University until the city was silent. She kept her light off and pretended she was out to all who knocked and hollered at her door. She trusted no one. In the daylight hours she scribbled pages about everything she had seen up until then, determined that some record of this Chuldur family, their habits, their movements and their dangers would exist.

When she was finally rescued from her dead city, she had to be dragged out of her office by force. Despite being taken to safety, she remained in a state of mistrust. She flinched at every being who spoke to her, never sure if they were the same person twice. To this day she remains in solitary confinement, recorded as the lone survivor of the Capriskia City Collapse and a possible Chuldur.

Her papers were entered into record with her plea that they be made public. This was in the hope that the next place visited by a Chuldur would be better able to defend itself.

That someone would be able to stop them.

Chapter 23
A Terrible Match

Ruby knew what she should be doing right now: she should be in the ballroom waiting for the return of the Doctor and Rogue. That was what they'd agreed.

She had watched the Duchess scurry out after them, so the bait part of the plan had worked. The Doctor and Rogue probably already had her and were relying on Ruby to keep everyone safe inside the ballroom until the alien murderer was dealt with. People and history saved.

However, what no one had accounted for in this plan was the absolute untethered chaos of a person who has a crush and the lengths someone will go to in this scenario.

What they hadn't accounted for was Miss Emily Beckett.

When the Duchess had left the ballroom, she had stopped on her way out to whisper to Lord Barton. Then he turned on his heel and followed her. This action had pushed Emily over the edge. She was in pieces about the danger her precious Lord Barton might have been walking towards and rushed after him.

Which was how Ruby found herself no longer helping the Doctor and instead chasing after her new friend, as she played 'Find the Lord' throughout the massive mansion – an unexpected parlour game they didn't have time for.

'He's not up here either,' cried Emily as she opened and slammed bedroom doors in the upstairs corridor. 'I have to warn him!'

Ruby moved as quickly as she could down the corridor, holding her side. Running about after eating all those finger sandwiches had given her a stitch. This was not something acknowledged in TV shows, she reflected. She turned into a bedroom doorway and found Emily, leaning dramatically against a window, a picture of despair.

'The Doctor won't let your lord get hurt,' Ruby said. 'Whether he deserves it or not. He cares about everyone.'

Emily shot Ruby a sharp glare. 'You don't understand. I know him. The *real* him,' she insisted. 'He likes to play the rake but deep down he's a romantic, searching for his perfect match. If only he knew, it's always been me!' She bowed her head and wafted her fan in front of her face, clearly in an attempt to prevent herself from further crying.

Ruby sighed and leaned against the windowpane next to her. It wasn't that she didn't care about Emily's pain; she had just hoped that an alien on a killing spree would take priority on this occasion.

'You can't make someone love you,' she said. 'You need to find someone who likes you, for you. Someone who doesn't make you chase them all over a house.'

Emily gave a shuddering breath. 'I know, you're right. I've been so silly.' She stood up and smoothed back her hair, giving Ruby an apologetic smile. Then her face changed to amazement as she spotted something through the window. 'He's outside!'

Ruby rolled her eyes and got up. She could see Lord Barton on the patio below, lit by the glow of the lamps in the garden.

He wasn't alone. He was chatting to some other figures next to him, but she couldn't see who.

Why were they all outside? Hadn't the Doctor and Rogue headed that way with the Chuldur? Ruby turned to confer with Emily but she was gone. After one glimpse of her beloved, Emily had already abandoned her resolve and was running downstairs to join him.

'Emily, wait!' she called out. But Emily either didn't hear her, or didn't want to.

As Ruby followed her friend downstairs, she was overcome with a sinking feeling that running towards Lord Barton was a very bad idea. Where was the Doctor when she needed him?

Chapter 24
The Chuldur

The patio of Pemberton Manor had been graced with many socialites in its time – earls, baronesses and even a famous poet or two. The Partrian family of Chuldur and their associates, however, were its first extraplanetary visitors.

While their outfits remained fitting for the period, their faces were feathered and bird-like. For the human Chuldur-watchers amongst you, they looked a lot like the following birds:

The Duchess's face was reminiscent of a southern cassowary, with a deep blue turkey neck, red veins, red beak and turquoise forehead. She had a streak of brown feathers across the top of her head, as if she wore a crown; she definitely considered herself worthy of one.

Lord Frampton had a kākāpō-like head, puffy green and yellow feathers all over his face with a long beak drooping down the middle, giving him a 'sad clown' expression. He nervously hopped from foot to foot, feeling sure he was about to get shouted at for something. He was often right.

Miss Talbot, next to him, had the large, surprised eyes of a king vulture, with light purple feathers across her face. She had a dark beak beneath orange nostril flaps, which made it almost look as if her beak were decorated with a bow. Her arms were a weird mix of long evening gloves, feathers and claws because she struggled with camouflage when she got excited.

The Butler was auklet-like, with grey feathers and white designer stripes on the sides of his face and around his eyes. He had a bright orange beak with a curly tuft of feathers sprouting out the top of it, like his beak had a question mark over it and should more accurately be called 'a beak?' He wriggled uncomfortably in his human outfit, as though it didn't quite fit.

Lord Barton was the only one to have reverted to the human form he had taken, aware that they were close to the manor and the human guests were inside.

The Chuldur had returned to the manor full of disappointment at their unsuccessful hunt.

The Duchess, the eldest sister of the Partrian family, was looking about for someone to blame. 'The Doctor and the other one have seen what we are. Now there'll be panic and screaming. It will ruin the authenticity of the evening.'

'I like the panic and screaming bit,' said Miss Talbot, her younger sister. 'I can always spot a fainter.' She clapped her claws together, excited at the thought.

The Butler, their cousin, shook off his bird form. His human face was equally pouty. 'If we're moving things up, I want to change. I'm sick of this. Not one person has accused me of murder.'

'I told you, wrong era,' Miss Talbot groaned at him. It wasn't the first time the Butler had complained about this.

Lord Barton stepped up to address the group. He had attended enough Partrian family events to know when things were about to get messy, and he didn't want to see the whole night go to ruin. 'Friends, please! This is what we came for – gossip, romance, scandal. The full Regency experience. There's still fun to be had.'

The Duchess's yellow eyes glared at him, unconvinced, but Lord Frampton moved next to Barton, nervously taking his side.

'I agree! I was promised excitement. I'm not killing everyone until I'm the source of at least one rumour.'

'Maybe *I* should faint,' Miss Talbot said, brushing back her feathers and turning to look hopefully at the Duchess. As the host of the event, she set the location and theme, so it was only polite for her to decide when to decimate it.

'Darling, then we'll go to London.' Lord Barton took the Duchess's hand and kissed it, a cheeky glint in his human eyes. 'I've heard there's a royal family to play with. Don't let the Doctor ruin our games.'

The Duchess nodded. *Royalty!* He could tell that she had liked that. He had joined the group initially because of his sister – but she wasn't that fun. Even so, the Duchess held the most power in the group and Lord Barton found himself pulled towards it. To her.

The Duchess clicked her beak and said, 'We will advance with the wedding. That'll get them out of hiding.' She took her claw out of Barton's and the way she smiled at him, he knew: the fun would continue. 'We can play our games on a magnificent scale! Parliament first, and then royalty! Oh, we're going to cosplay this planet to death!'

Cheering and chirping with joy on the patio, they were completely unaware of the sound of footsteps rushing down towards them.

It was only the scream of Emily Beckett that made them turn around.

Lord Barton saw Emily and thought, *I'll deal with her later, snore, boring.* In the present, he had a more urgent matter and some unfinished business to attend to.

Now, finally, he could kill Ruby Sunday.

Ruby took one look at the group of Chuldur on the patio and the monstrous, bird-like face of the Duchess and knew what came next. She grabbed Emily's hand and ran. No time to explain, no time to stop. She had to find the Doctor.

She pulled them back into the manor, her brain trying to focus on something practical to drown out the fear. Too scared to say out loud what was really on her mind – *What's happened to the Doctor and Rogue?*

Inside, they pushed past the guests in the entrance hall. Beside her, Emily gasped and Ruby turned: Lord Barton was now behind them, weaving his way through the crowd, smiling at them both.

'Oh, ladies,' he cooed after them. It was sinister.

Emily whimpered again. 'What is he, what monster?' she continued to cry. 'What nightmare?'

Ruby held on to her hand, pulling her as far away from Barton as she could manage. 'I'm sorry, Emily. I don't think he's Lord Barton any more.'

But her words weren't comfort enough. With a big sob, Emily let go of Ruby's hand and ran down the hallway, knocking some guests against the punchbowl as she went.

'Emily!' Ruby called after her, trying to keep her voice hushed so they'd not be heard by Barton or any of the other Chuldur.

Luckily, Emily was a creature of habit, and Ruby saw her run into a familiar doorway. Back into the dimly lit library in which they'd first met.

Inside, she found Emily sobbing among the shelving stacks. Ruby crouched down next to her. She peered out over the books, keeping her eyes on the door, listening for any sign of approach.

At least they were hidden for now.

Emily turned away, fanning herself furiously. Her breathing was ragged, terrified.

Ruby felt for her. She remembered the disbelief, confusion and panic she'd felt the first time she'd seen and fought the extraordinary aspects of the universe. *Not everyone wants to see*, she thought, *and not everyone can cope when they do.*

'I'm sorry, Emily, I know it's hard. There are scary things out there in the universe, but I promise you, the good things outnumber them.'

Emily looked up at Ruby, and stopped crying for a moment, curious. 'How do you know all these things?'

When travelling through time you try not to disturb people's world views, but Ruby figured at this point Emily had been through enough. She deserved the truth. 'Because I'm not from your time and place. I'm from the future.'

Emily's eyes widened in amazement as she moved closer to Ruby. 'You are truly remarkable. I thought I was interesting, a bookish wallflower risking it all for a secret love.'

Ruby didn't answer, keeping watch on the library door, unsure how long they could hide there.

'But you...' Emily continued. 'You live a life of adventure, danger, travelling through time, helping your friends.'

Ruby noticed a shimmer of blue light against the bookcase but by the time she turned back, it was too late to run. All she had time to take in was Emily's face being suddenly engulfed by bright turquoise feathers. The red beak and the red feathers that had just appeared beneath her chin were like splashes of blood dripping down her neck.

The final image of her life would be watching her friend morph into the creature that would kill her.

'So why stay this bookish wallflower,' Emily said, her now clawed hand grabbing Ruby's wrist, 'when I could be you?'

Chapter 25
The Escape

'Where are you going?' Rogue heard the Doctor say as he marched briskly ahead in the garden, their clothes drying in the cool night air. The manor was ahead, but Rogue wasn't walking that way. He had expected one Chuldur, that was the contract. Not a family. He'd counted at least five. These were very bad odds.

'I'm not being paid enough for this.'

'Paid or not, people have died.' The Doctor had his sonic screwdriver out and he was fiddling with the waterlogged trap while they walked. Rogue thought he was as focused on fixing machines as Art had been. Annoyingly, both of them had the ability to do that and argue at the same time.

'We go back there, *we'll* die,' Rogue insisted.

'So you'll just walk away?'

Rogue stopped. He could see a few Chuldur outside on the manor patio. He turned sharply and pulled the Doctor behind a row of trees. He peered out, hoping they hadn't been spotted. It looked like they were changing back into human form and going back inside.

Rogue had read about a family of Chuldur. One that had destroyed every place it visited, leaving no survivors. In the past, he would have dived headlong into this kind of danger without batting an eyelid. He loved the rush of adrenalin and he had that stubborn will to reach his target, whatever it took. Then he had suffered the cost.

The Doctor was wrong. He wouldn't just walk away from all this.

He'd run.

'There's too many. It's not my problem.' Rogue quickened his pace away from the manor and towards the *Yossarian*. This time, the Doctor did not follow him. He had stopped still, determined not to take another step. Rogue reluctantly stopped too and turned back to face him.

'If it's not our problem, whose is it?' The Doctor's voice was cold, angry. 'Who do you think will help these people if we don't? You're here. You've seen what they're doing. You are *choosing* not to care.'

In the dark garden, Rogue stood defiantly across from the Doctor, his breath shallow and fast. He'd hit a nerve. Rogue had had years of practice at not caring and didn't want to change now. The Doctor was calm in comparison, determined and immovable.

Rogue knew that if he chose to walk away now, he would be walking away alone.

He looked out across the fields, towards the *Yossarian* and the tree that had barely hidden the Doctor's magnificent shed. Then he gave a sigh and looked back at the Doctor, gesturing at the trap.

'Even if you get it working, it's too small. What's the plan? Trap one while the others kill us?'

The Doctor gave a satisfied smile as he started walking towards the manor. Okay, he'd won the argument this time. Rogue just hoped they'd survive long enough for him to win next time. The Doctor's sonic made clicking, whirring noises as he pressed it against the trap. 'All it needs is a little bit of zizz.'

'Zizz?'

'Technical term. I can make this transport carry four.'

'There were five.' The Doctor pressed the screwdriver against the trap once more and jiggled it. 'There – five, maybe six, maximum. Problem is, too much weight. Now it can only work once.'

The odds were getting worse.

When they reached the patio, the Chuldur were gone. Rogue and the Doctor moved to the side of the building and slid open a ground-floor window. The Doctor was about to clamber through when Rogue reached for his hand.

'Are you sure?' Rogue asked, his voice soft.

They were facing beings that had destroyed cities, taken countless lives. How could the two of them stop such creatures? And with one shot? He felt a deep ache in his chest; he couldn't lose someone else.

Rogue looked pleadingly at the Doctor. If he gave himself enough time and distance, he could learn to forget his troubles and bury his guilt. He could stop himself from caring. Rogue had done it before. He could do it again.

He could show the Doctor how.

'We could go anywhere,' he said.

'I'm going in here,' replied the Doctor. Not a waver in his voice, not a second of doubt.

Rogue looked into the Doctor's eyes and knew that he would never stop caring. Could never stop wanting to help, to fight, to go on. That was who he was.

The Doctor let go of Rogue's hand and climbed in through the window, and Rogue did what he knew he would do for ever.

Follow him.

Chapter 26
The Host

The Duchess was through with hiding.

Resplendent in her gown and with her Chuldur face on show, she pushed open the ballroom doors. In human form her dress had been a bit much, but now the floral pattern really brought out the glowing yellow in her eyes. She felt positively radiant as the string quartet screeched to a halt and the guests started to scream.

'Attention, s'il vous plaît, merci, wilkommen and bienvenue, c'est moi! Come now, loves, a party isn't a party without a costume change, and don't I look *fabulous*?' she practically squawked as she marched into the centre of the ballroom, flanked by Miss Talbot and the Butler, also in Chuldur form. The crowd rushed to the edges of the room, panicked.

The consensus of the room seemed to be that the Duchess's new look was terrifying.

'Now it's time to toast the person who made tonight possible.' The Duchess grabbed a glass of champagne off a trembling servant's tray and raised it aloft. 'Me!'

The guests were clearly still in shock, so she tried again. 'Rude. A toast … to ME!' she snapped in the face of a colonel, who promptly fainted.

Miss Talbot gleefully leant in to the butler. 'See, there's always a fainter.'

Up above, the Doctor and Rogue had snuck onto the balcony, watching the scene below. The Doctor thought Rogue had been right from the beginning, this was the best vantage point. Behind the Duchess, he saw Lord Frampton shoving the remaining guests into the ballroom and locking the doors behind them.

'This is the endgame,' Rogue whispered. 'They'll leave no witnesses, no survivors.'

'Any sign of Ruby?'

Rogue shook his head.

There were murmurs of fear from the guests on the floor below.

'SILENCE!' shouted the Duchess. 'Darlings, it has been my absolute pleasure to host you tonight, but now it is time for us to get to ... the season finale! And what could be better than a wedding?' She stomped her feet at the bewildered crowd. 'I said there's going to be a wedding. Gasp and whisper, please!'

The crowd did their best to react as the Duchess wanted, clearly afraid of upsetting the monster in front of them.

The Doctor was not deterred, as he counted the Chuldur he could see. Four, their bird-faces the same as before. That left Lord Barton unaccounted for. If this wedding was their big end event, he was running out of time. However, it did provide one thing in his favour.

The Doctor handed Rogue the trap. 'We'll wait until they're all together. We've got one try at this, Rogue. Just one. And we've got to get it right, first time.'

Beneath them the Duchess nodded, satisfied by the forced gasps and whispers of the crowd. 'Better.'

The Doctor marvelled at how the Duchess could still believe she was commanding respect when all she instilled in people was fear.

At the far end of the hall, Lord Frampton opened the doors to let in the last two guests.

'And here is the happy couple!' the Duchess said, delighted.

The crowd turned to see Lord Barton enter the room. His face altered from Chuldur form back to human, showing off for the crowd. The Doctor was not surprised. This was the big finale, so of course Lord Barton would be the groom. There would also be a bride, which meant there must be six Chuldur in total, not five. All he needed was to wait for the full wedding party to be in place.

Lord Barton held out his hand as his bride stepped in to join him. In that second, all the Doctor's anticipation vanished and was replaced with despair.

It was Ruby. She clasped Lord Barton's hand as he paraded her through the ballroom like a prize. Her other hand was gently waving a fan in front of face, exactly as her friend Emily had done so often before.

Ruby smiled at the terrified crowd, as if enjoying their attention. Spread out amongst the guests, the other Chuldur applauded her arrival. This was the occasion they had been waiting for.

The Duchess approached the couple and prodded at Ruby's skin, a little put out. 'You know I wanted to wear that.'

'I got there first!' gloated Ruby as she gave her new outfit a proud twirl.

She looks exactly like Ruby, the Doctor thought, *but she isn't Ruby any more. She's a Chuldur.* He sank back on the balcony, unable to control his breathing, his two hearts beating furiously.

Down below, there was a skirmish in the crowd as one of the guests, Mr Price the vicar, was dragged forward by Miss Talbot and shoved towards the Duchess.

'Madam. Your Grace. Your… Birdiness. I'm sorry, but this flies in the face of all my teachings.' The vicar put his hands up, begging the Duchess for mercy. 'I cannot sanction wedlock for creatures from Hell.'

The butler stepped forward proudly. 'Oh, I get to murder after all!' He giggled as he dashed across the floor towards the vicar and grabbed the man's face with his claw. There was a crackle of electricity, and a flash of blue light filled the hall – followed by a THUD as the vicar fell to the floor.

Dead.

The butler turned to the crowd, letting out an awful shriek, clearly pleased with his new outfit. His face was still in its Chuldur form, but his body was that of the vicar, the husk of the real vicar lying at his feet. The crowd screamed once more.

Up on the balcony the Doctor could no longer contain himself. He stepped forward defiantly, fuelled by rage. But Rogue had already wrapped an arm around his chest and hauled him backwards out of the room.

Chapter 27
Carla

The Doctor struggled as Rogue pulled him into the upstairs corridor. Then he closed his eyes and held still.

'Sorry,' said Rogue, loosening his grip, 'but if they catch us, we save no one.'

The Doctor knew he was right but he couldn't stop his thoughts...

Not her.

Please, not her.

'Do they *have* to kill to become somebody else?' he asked, searching for hope.

Rogue just looked at him sadly and nodded.

This can't be it, thought the Doctor. *There has to be a way.*

Did it hurt her when it happened?

'There must be a way to reverse the process,' said the Doctor. 'We'll capture her. Take her somewhere, to someone who can find a piece of her in there, something we can use to bring her back.' He was desperate, and Rogue's silence gave him every answer he didn't want.

Rogue slowly opened his arms, and the Doctor fell into them and sobbed. 'I'm sorry,' Rogue said over and over.

But this barely registered as reality swam around the Doctor and meaning didn't matter any more.

He looked ahead into nothing. Numb.

A voice called out in the nothing.

'Doctor!'

'Doctor, look...'

It was a brilliant, sunny morning in Ruby's London flat. This was long before the Chuldur, long before much at all had happened.

The Doctor was sitting in the small but welcoming kitchen with Ruby's mum, Carla. Two cups of tea were steaming in front of them.

Down the hallway they could hear bangs and clatters, the sounds of Ruby frantically packing a suitcase.

'I'll just be a minute,' her voice rang out as Carla looked at the Doctor, worried.

'Doctor, look, you know I can't stop her, and I wouldn't want to do that …' She stopped, composing herself. 'And if anyone deserves to see it all, feel it all, it's Ruby.'

The Doctor smiled at her. He couldn't agree more.

'But I'm still her mum. I need to know she'll be okay.' She paused. 'You'll keep her safe?'

The Doctor took her hand in his, reassuringly. 'I'll keep her safe.'

Back leaning on Rogue's shoulder, this promise went round and round in his mind.

I've failed her.

Then a more powerful voice silenced the sad chorus in his thoughts.

We aren't leaving without a fight.

The Doctor stepped back from Rogue but kept his head down, still recovering. 'How long do they live?' he asked quietly.

'Chuldur? They have a lifespan of 600 years,' replied Rogue.

'Good' said the Doctor, a furious anger rising in his chest. 'That's a long time to suffer.'

Chapter 28
The Wedding

The Chuldur leader, playing the Duchess, considered herself the greatest host of any Chuldur event. Each one had been unique, daring and, above all, fun.

When she was younger, she had watched show after show of courtroom thrillers, period dramas and, of course, Urbankan murder mysteries. Whatever the location, she was thrilled to see so much romance, intrigue and generally a lot happening to people in an inordinately short space of time.

In comparison, her own life seemed slow and uneventful so she had decided, very early on, that her future would be as exciting as any TV show. She would take the lives of many and spin it all into a brilliant drama.

Now, that would be living.

Recently, she had been inspired by *Bridgerton*, all eight seasons and spin-offs. The group had grown large enough now for such ensemble-based stories, and their power in numbers meant they could be a little less cautious with their typical party plans. And it wasn't as if anyone in this time could ring for help and tell anyone what they'd seen.

Communication devices had been an annoying issue in Capriskia City; too much had been said about the Chuldur and their LARPing about. Luckily, false rumours spread just as fast when you played authority figures and called them facts. They learnt their lesson that day, though: no one in this room was getting out alive. Then it would be off to play at Buckingham Palace in London. Same era. Same thrills. She could feel the crown on her head now.

Before this, though, she had a wedding to organise. The other Chuldur looked to her and expected the highest of standards. She would not disappoint.

She had ordered the vicar's corpse to be swept away, behind the flower arrangements. It didn't fit with the colour scheme. Then she had directed Lord Barton to stand at the far end of the hall in the makeshift stage area, with Ruby at the other, following the correct Earth customs. She might have been planning to kill her audience, but they wouldn't leave this Earth without a good view.

The guests had been corralled into two groups, bride and groom, creating an aisle down the centre of the room. She did think it a shame that the crowd looked so scared now; she had envisaged this as a joyous occasion.

'Please, do stop your whimpering. Big smiles!' she hissed at them through her beak. 'In the tedium of your lives, this should be a thrilling day. Act like it.'

Some of the guests offered tense smiles back, but they weren't convincing. The Duchess could tell she needed to persuade them further. 'Anyone else want to change?' she enquired of her family, prompting audible cries from the terrified guests.

Lord Frampton stepped eagerly towards a grey-haired gentleman in a gold waistcoat. 'What about a father of the bride?'

'Can we all stop messing about, please?' Ruby interrupted. 'It's my wedding, and I want the Duchess to give me away.' She looked pointedly at the Duchess, who gave her a mocking curtsey. Her middle sister really was annoying, even more so since Lord Barton had begun travelling with their group, but she was, on this occasion, right. The Duchess *had* to be in the wedding party.

The Duchess waved for the others to take their positions. She leaned over the string quartet, who were sat back behind their instruments. 'Play something romantic!'

They started playing, their hands shaking, as Ruby took the Duchess's arm and started her slow march down the aisle.

Everything was perfect. Lord Barton stood by the Chuldur-faced vicar, the picture of a handsome beau awaiting his true love. In front of Ruby walked Miss Talbot, who was already dabbing her eyes – the perfect bridesmaid but so emotional. The guests at the front flinched as Lord Frampton joined their row and prepared to object to the union. Every good wedding needs an objection, the Duchess felt. Even the crowd seemed appropriately tearful.

Ruby walked arm in arm with the Duchess, batting that silly fan of hers. If the Duchess wasn't mistaken, she even seemed a little nervous, silly goose.

This was the problem with her middle sister. She took the parts too much to heart.

She needed reminding that anything said during the drama was just play-acting.

The Duchess vowed that at her next event she would have a fling with Barton, just to help her sister realise that their marriage was bogus.

Anything to help a family member.

She handed Ruby over to Lord Barton then moved over to the side to watch. Lord Barton looked incredibly smug as he took Ruby's hand. 'I always knew we would end up together.'

Ruby gave him a fiery look. 'No one else would put up with you.'

The Duchess gave a little snort. Maybe they weren't such a happy couple after all.

The vicar started the proceedings. 'Dearly beloved, we are gathered here for the wedding of Lord Barton and er ...' He grasped for Ruby's name, and the Duchess rolled her eyes. Honestly, why did her cousin take a role if he couldn't do it well? It was like he was playing the chef at Traxos all over again; if she hadn't turned his food-poisoning debacle into an assassination attempt, the whole night would have been ruined.

'Lady Ruby Sunday,' the Duchess interjected with a cold stare.

'Lady Ruby Sunday! Thank you ...'

The Duchess was trying her best to get into the moment but, now the service had actually started, everything felt a little benign. Maybe it was because the crowd knew they were Chuldur; maybe it was because her night felt cut short. She'd wanted more time to make a spectacle of the Duchess, to have her big moment. It felt odd that the audience were all staring at the couple; she did prefer it when they stared at her. Still, they were getting up to her favourite part of any wedding story, the objection. She looked eagerly at Lord Frampton. Any moment now ...

'Lord Barton,' the vicar began. 'Do you—'

There was an almighty BANG as the doors to the ballroom exploded open and in walked the Doctor, putting the sonic in his pocket.

'I object! Had we got to that part yet? It's hard to hear from out there.'

Well, thought the Duchess, *this is a delightful twist. No one from the current time-frame could make that kind of entrance. This is no ordinary physician – and how courteous of him to return to me.*

She knew instantly: she had to *be* him.

It looked as if she'd get her big moment after all.

Chapter 29
The Objection

The Doctor milked his walk down the aisle for everything it was worth. This was his moment to shine and, as he stepped through an exploded door and struck one hell of a pose, how could he not?

He wanted every Chuldur in the room to see him and want to be him. That way they'd stop killing everyone else and just focus on him.

The hard part, of course, would be stopping them from killing him immediately. It wasn't a perfect plan, he decided, as he stopped halfway down the aisle and gave the crowd a wave.

The Duchess licked her beak in anticipation.

'I object to this wedding,' the Doctor announced. 'And to everything you are, Chuldur.'

He could see all the Chuldur in the wedding party at the front of the crowd. Some of them had already discarded their human disguises, and they clicked their beaks as the Duchess moved in front of them, looking him up and down.

'We're just having a bit of fun, Doctor.' She took another step towards him. 'So we gate-crashed a party. We're clearly not the only ones.'

'Yeah, I don't need an invite. Because I'm owning this.' He did a spin on one foot for the crowd. 'Take me in, baby, I'm one of a kind.' He saw the other Chuldur move forward to stare down the aisle, transfixed by the new alien at the party.

'He's not human!' declared Lord Frampton, the last to catch up.

Miss Talbot clapped excitedly. 'He is something unknown. I want to be him, I want, I want!'

She gave a loud caw and blue light crackled as she stepped towards the Doctor. There were shrieks from the crowd.

The Duchess grabbed her arm and pulled her back into the group. 'Now, now, sister. Maybe someone else would like this delight.'

The Doctor watched her move to the head of the group, making sure none of them could get past her.

Looks like the Duchess is killing me tonight, he thought.

'Fascinating,' she said, looking the Doctor up and down admiringly. 'A traveller like us.'

'Yeah, but no thanks, not like you.' The Doctor pulled an exaggerated, disgusted face. 'Never like you. I travel to see life, in all its amazing variation. The people, the places. You? You leave a trail of pain and destruction everywhere you go. Selfishly taking lives instead of getting one of your own. And all for a bit of fun. If you can call this fun.'

The Duchess's feathers were visibly ruffled. 'Watch your tone, Doctor.'

'Don't think I will. Sorry, loves, your fun stops now. It's time to run.'

The Duchess laughed at him, looking about the room. 'Oh my dear, why would we run? We clearly outnumber you.'

'I wasn't talking to you.'

The Doctor looked at the crowd of guests, clinging together, terrified and very confused by the stand-off happening in front of them. He gestured at the open doors behind him, 'My big entrance, also your big exit. RUN!' He was continually surprised by the number of times you had to tell people that.

With their newly gained permission, the guests fled in droves through the door, creating a flurry of noise and movement through the ballroom. The Doctor stood perfectly still, staring at the Chuldur, a pillar of calm amongst a sea of panic.

The Chuldur looked unsure what to do – chase the guests or stay for a chance to be the Doctor. As he'd hoped, they all stayed put. To the family who could not share, he was just too delicious as bait. Now the innocent partygoers were safe, he raised his head high, ready for the final showdown.

'I appreciate your sense of drama, Doctor. Really, I *love* it.' A blue light started to crackle out from the Duchess; she wasn't going to wait any longer. He had seconds, maybe. A vexil, tops.

'Oh, I know. You live for the drama. That's why you couldn't resist me storming in here, delaying your wedding, causing a scene.' The Doctor spread his arms, enjoying his centre-stage moment in the now empty ballroom. 'But unlike you, I didn't do it for entertainment. I did it so you'd look at me. Not at *him*.'

The Chuldur frowned in confusion, as a small metallic object shot out from behind them, skimming along the ballroom floor to land by the Doctor's foot. It was a piece of Rogue's trap.

The Chuldur turned and saw Rogue. He'd already laid the other two parts of the trap on the floor, and now the Doctor had the third. They formed a perfect triangle around the Chuldur.

Rogue gave them a cheeky wave as he declared, 'Triform on.'

A brilliant glowing white light zipped between the pieces of the trap, as the floor beneath the Chuldur's feet became a white-glowing triangle.

The Chuldur shrieked and cawed as they tried to move. Wriggling and blue-light crackling but it was no use. They could not escape.

'You will pay for this, Doctor!' The Duchess spat out her words towards him, shaking with rage.

'If you want me to pay, you'll have to hurry. A Transport Gate with six passengers gives you about –' he glanced over at Rogue – 'sixty vexils?'

Rogue nodded. 'Sounds about right.'

They shared a satisfied look as the Doctor got the trigger mechanism out of his top pocket, ready to press send. They'd done it.

'How long's a vexil?' asked the false Ruby. She sounded worried, sincere.

The Doctor found it hard to look at her face. 'Oh, don't pretend,' he said.

'I'm not. Doctor. It's me.'

The words slammed through the Doctor's whole body. For the first time since he'd entered the room, the Doctor looked into Ruby's eyes. He had wanted to end this without seeing her like this. He wanted to remember her how she was, his amazing, brilliantfriend who brought out the best in everyone. Brought out the best in him.

'My mum's called Carla and my gran's called Cherry, and we met space babies, and I'm really, really sorry.' There were tears in Ruby's eyes.

The Doctor took a sharp intake of breath. These weren't the fake tears of a Chuldur playing with feelings or the angry tears of a thwarted enemy. These were the real, scared tears of his best friend, telling him she was still there. 'But how?'

Ruby gave him an apologetic shrug. 'I cosplayed.'

Chapter 30
The Fate of Ruby Sunday

'So why stay this bookish wallflower when I could be you?'

Ruby's eyes widened in fear, seeing Emily's true face as the Chuldur gripped her by her wrist, ready to drain the life out of her. Behind her, Ruby felt the large bookcase, penning her in.

She was going to die in this library if she didn't think of something fast.

So she thought of something fast.

She raised her free hand to her ear. She tapped the psychic earrings twice.

'Battle mode!' Ruby said loud and clear.

The earrings took control of her body.

There was a loud CRACK as Ruby threw Emily into a bookcase.

Wooden shards and books flew everywhere and Emily landed in a heap on the rug in front of the fire.

She gave a grunt as she dragged herself up, and Ruby could see a look of surprise on her face.

The earrings guided Ruby's handspring over the demolished bookcase, and she landed with a neat curtsey on the rug in front of the Chuldur.

Emily's silk gloves promptly morphed into long, sharp bird-like claws. Her suddenly feathered arms swiped at Ruby, left and right. She lunged forward, still lashing out, but Ruby somehow ducked and pirouetted out of every attack.

Emily shrieked in frustration, picked up a nearby bookshelf and hurled it at Ruby.

Ruby felt herself jump out of the way and roll onto the floor. The bookshelf crashed next to her, millimetres from her face. She quickly backflipped to her feet again, fists ready.

Oh, she really loved psychic earrings.

Emily picked up a wooden shard from the floor. It had previously been a ladder rung but now looked more like a spike. She gripped her makeshift weapon in her claw and advanced on Ruby, her eyes glinting with that blue glow.

Ruby knew she was fast, but Emily was stronger than her and it didn't look like she would give up anytime soon. Ruby backed towards a further row of bookcases and she looked around her for some defence.

Then she saw something, on the floor.

Emily raised the jagged stake above her head and leapt towards Ruby, stabbing downwards, with force.

Ruby spun out of the way, reaching a hand for the floor. When she sprang back up, her own weapon was ready. Clutched in her hand was something called *Virtue Rewarded* by Pamela Somebody. Ruby swung the heavy tome into Emily's side and sent her flying into the row of remaining bookcases. As Emily hit the first one, the others wobbled and then fell like dominos.

There was a scream from Emily as they all crashed down on top of her. Then silence.

From the floor, Ruby could see the bookcases were not moving. Emily was trapped somewhere underneath. She threw her book on top of them and exclaimed, 'Nowt wrong with being bookish.'

She turned off battle mode and crept quietly to the door, opening it a fraction. Down the corridor, she could see Lord Barton walking in her direction, checking rooms, the Butler and Miss Talbot not far behind him. Looking for her.

She needed to buy time to find the Doctor. But how?

Ruby looked behind her and saw a lone item, left on the rug by the fireplace.

Emily's fan.

She must have dropped it in the fight.

The footsteps outside were getting closer. Ruby swiped the fan from the floor and exited the library. Lord Barton looked startled to see her approach.

Ruby waved Emily's fan in front of her face and gave him an adoring smile. 'What do you think of my new look?'

Chapter 31
The Trap

Rogue smiled. The plan had worked. The Doctor had distracted the Chuldur, and the fleeing crowd had provided the perfect cover for him to weave through them, arriving unnoticed behind the Chuldur.

As he placed down the first piece of the trap it made a click and he felt sure the Chuldur would turn, see him, kill him. But no. He crept quietly behind them and placed down piece two, ready to skim the third to the Doctor.

His role complete, Rogue gave a nod and watched the Doctor showboat as they trapped them all in one go. Their one chance had paid off, and they'd done the job with style. Rogue had to admit, he'd even enjoyed it. He was used to catching his target; saving the day, that was new.

He liked it.

It was a lifestyle he could get used to.

Then Ruby spoke, and Rogue saw the Doctor crumble. She wasn't Chuldur. He'd trapped his friend in with these monsters. Waiting for the Gate to charge so he could send them on their one-way trip to a barren nowhere, lost deep within the stars. Now Ruby was trapped with them, and they only had sixty vexils to decide what to do about it.

Rogue tried to think of any words that might help console him. Before he could say anything, they were presented with another issue.

There was an angry caw from the doorway. Miss Emily Beckett had arrived. She was in Chuldur form. Her turquoise feathers stood askew at angles, and her red beak was bent and twisted to one side.

The Duchess looked over at her, perplexed. 'What on earth happened to you?'

Emily snapped her beak back into position with a grunt before pointing at Ruby. 'She happened!'

In a fit of fury, Emily charged at Ruby, running foolishly into the triangle and becoming immediately stuck to the floor. Claws outstretched, she struggled to reach Ruby, swiping inches from the girl's face.

'What is this?' Emily cried as the Duchess gave a frustrated yelp.

'A trap!' said the Duchess furiously.

Emily thrashed about, but it was no good. She looked from Lord Barton to Ruby and the vicar. 'Were you going to marry her?!'

Lord Barton looked sheepish. 'I thought she was you!'

'But how could you mistake *her* for *me*?' shrieked Emily.

'She has the scent of a Chuldur.'

'It's a false scent,' the Duchess realised. 'From that cheap psychic jewellery!'

There could only be thirty vexils left, if that, Rogue reckoned. The Doctor hadn't taken his eyes off Ruby. The trap flickered under the weight of its seventh inhabitant.

How many had the Doctor said it would hold – maybe six?

'Doctor, we only have one chance,' Rogue said, moving close to him, seeing the look of agony on his face. 'Remember?'

'I can't do it,' the Doctor implored. 'It'll send Ruby with *them*.'

'He's too much of a coward!' said the Duchess, looking satisfied. 'Where are you sending us, Doctor? I can't imagine it's anywhere nice. But at least you'll be giving us one toy to play with.'

Emily swiped at Ruby again. 'She's mine!'

The glowing triangle of the trap flickered, and Emily managed a slight step towards Ruby. She looked excitedly at her prey.

Rogue eyed the trap anxiously. It was starting to break down.

From the trap, the automated voice announced, 'Transport Gate charged. Press send in ten vexils.'

The countdown had started.

Nine . . .

Rogue stepped closer to the Doctor. 'You have to activate at zero. If you don't, the Chuldur will escape and Ruby dies anyway.'

'But . . .'

Eight . . .

'Doctor, it's okay.' Ruby gave the Doctor a small nod. She clearly understood the cost if he didn't and was willing to accept her fate bravely.

A look of unbearable pain crossed the Doctor's face. The trap flickered once more as it continued to count down.

Seven…

Rogue didn't want to push him, but they were running out of time. 'They'll kill us, then everyone here. They'll destroy this world.'

Six…

Rogue was next to the Doctor now. He could hear him breathing hard. 'And you know that, you absolutely know that.' All that torment was wrapped so tight around his chest that Rogue could feel his heaviness, his dread. 'So, can you do it? Can you lose your friend to save the world?'

Five…

The Doctor started to cry. 'No.'

'I know.' Rogue smiled at the kind, brilliant, amazing man in front of him.

Four…

Then he stepped forward and wrapped the Doctor in his arms and kissed him. It was a soft, passionate kiss, full of promise.

The moment was tender. Romantic. It was theirs.

Three…

Rogue stepped back and gave the Doctor one last smile, revealing he had taken the trigger device from him. Then he turned quickly and ran full pelt into the trap.

Two...

It flicked on and off as the Chuldur tried to scramble to the edges. Emily moved a step towards Ruby, grabbing at her as Rogue barrelled in. He knocked Emily to the trap floor, causing Ruby to be thrown free. Only one shoe left behind.

One...

Rogue looked down at his feet inside the glowing triangle and back up to the Doctor. He was now trapped with the Chuldur, but he was not afraid.

Rogue could not have let the Doctor say goodbye to the person he was closest to. He knew that pain too well to let the Doctor hold it, even for a second. And so he'd known the decision he had to make.

He couldn't lose anyone else. But he was ready to be the one who was lost.

Zero.

'Find me,' Rogue said as he pressed send.

The patch of triangular floor turned jet black, as the Chuldur started to scream and fall.

Rogue caught a last glimpse of the Doctor before he dropped down into the darkness of the Transport Gate.

As he fell, his mind had one, clear thought.

Worth every second.

Chapter 32
Goodbye

The Doctor sat on the steps of the manor.

It was early morning now, and the gardens were awash in that brilliant blue dawn light. Everything felt incredibly still; the bumblebees were still sleeping, and the trees rocked in the breeze, barely awake themselves. The world continued to dance as if nothing had happened the night before.

The Doctor kept his eyes on the horizon as a gentle hum of machinery filled the air, and he watched the *Yossarian* take off into space. He would have been lost watching this if Ruby had not come and sat beside him.

'Just sending the ship into orbit around the moon, so it can wait for him.' He paused. 'As long as it takes.'

'Can't we use the TARDIS and go find him?'

'There are as many dimensions as there are atoms in the universe. Not impossible but… it's a bit impossible.'

The pair of them looked back up. The *Yossarian* was now a tiny speck in the sky, a forgotten star.

The Doctor laughed to himself. 'I don't even know his name.'

Ruby put her head on his shoulder and quietly said, 'I'm sorry.'

The Doctor just kept smiling, keeping his eyes on the sky. 'At least we got to live and love together a bit. Exist.' He moved away from Ruby, quickly; it was time to get on with things. 'Anyway, it is what it is, so onwards, fine. Next! Off we go, where shall we go? Anywhere!'

'Doctor you don't have to be like this—'

'I have to be like this because this is what I'm like. Onwards. Upwards. New horizons. New parties to be found. Moving on—'

'Okay, just shut up a second,' Ruby said. She grabbed him quickly and pulled him into a tight hug.

The Doctor leant into it and let himself feel what he had buried for a moment. Not all of it but just enough to carry on with the day.

'It's good to have you back, Ruby,' he said, nestled into her shoulder.

'And you, Doctor.'

The pair of them stepped apart and he gave Ruby a little twirl, one last dance for the road. She smiled.

The Doctor watched her head down the steps. His best friend. He was so happy she was here. That he had her back.

He was about to follow her, when he felt something. Something in his waistcoat pocket.

He reached inside and pulled out the object. Sitting in the middle of his palm was Rogue's gold ring. The one he had given him on the dancefloor. He smiled at it, letting it roll about his palm.

Then he popped it on his finger. It looked good.

A little piece of Rogue to go with him.

Chapter 33
The Forgotten Place

A *howl* in the darkness.

The wind growled ferociously around a barren and abandoned planet, far out in the forgotten reaches of space.

Giant grey rocks covered the surface. As the wind hit them, charcoal-sand blasted up, creating sandstorms wherever it hit. This was the only movement on the surface and, at first glance, it would have seemed the only sign of life. But if you looked more closely, there was a light.

From the mouth of a cave, the bright glow of a campfire burned through the grey.

Inside, sat a man.

Rogue.

He was trying to keep warm.

Rogue had been there for what felt like months. The cave had been a saviour, sheltering him from the environment but also from the enemies sent here with him. He had lost them, at least for now.

As time passed in the cave, any concept of a day had folded in on itself.

Rogue kept his mind busy with the simple tasks of staying alive: build the fire, watch the fire, build the fire again.

Rinse, repeat.

Thankfully, there was some food to be found on this planet – mainly winged dalnats and other small cave-dwelling creatures. But they were not enough. Rogue knew that if the cold didn't get him, starvation would.

What this planet didn't know, however, was that Rogue could not be broken so easily. He had made a promise to himself. He had agreed that he wasn't going to be lost any more.

Because Rogue had realised he was worth finding.

As the fire began to die, Rogue thought of the man he had come here for. The magnificent being who was beyond any comprehension of existence. The one known to most as the Doctor.

Of all the timelines they could both have inhabited, Rogue was grateful that their eyes had met on this one. What a great surprise that had been from the universe. Yes, right now, he was lonely, but time wasn't linear, and this was his favourite thing about it.

Rogue was sitting in this cave, but he was also walking with the Doctor in the garden, he was laughing with Art in the *Yossarian*, he was falling from a building, he was running from one memory of his life to another. All at once.

Rogue was in the Doctor's arms, spinning around and around, for ever.

Acknowledgements

A massive thank you and a hug to Russell T Davies for championing us. To Ncuti, Jonathan, Millie, Indira and the entire cast for bringing these characters to life in such a beautiful way. To the teams at BBC, Disney and Bad Wolf who made it possible for this book to exist – Scott Handcock and Ellen Marsh, you are treasures. Lastly, to our thrillingly wise and compassionate editor, Steve Cole, who even helped us write this bit.

From Briony: I would like to thank Andy Brereton and Kate Heggie for all the encouragement. Thanks also to the best human, Damian; my book-loving family; the robot-vampire Jake and Questing Time pals for the love, support and everything.

From Kate: I would like to thank my parents, for leaving me unmonitored to watch sci-fi/horror for hours as a child. I'd also like to thank my friends – Charlie Coombes, Zoe Alker, Emma McCleave and Becs Hyde – for being there, as well as the many, many people who have helped me along the way.

Lastly, we both thank *you* – our reader.

Thank you for reading our book.